JOHN BLACKBURN

A Sour Apple Tree

I0633551

VALANCOURT BOOKS

A Sour Apple Tree by John Blackburn
Originally published in Great Britain by Secker & Warburg in 1958
First U.S. edition published by Mill & Morrow in 1959
First Valancourt Books edition 2024

Published by Valancourt Books, Richmond, Virginia
http://www.valancourtbooks.com

ISBN 978-1-960241-32-0 (*trade paperback*)
Also available as an electronic book.

Set in Dante MT
Cover by Pedro Marques

A SOUR APPLE TREE

JOHN BLACKBURN was born in 1923 in the village of Corbridge, England, the second son of a clergyman. Blackburn attended Haileybury College near London beginning in 1937, but his education was interrupted by the onset of World War II; the shadow of the war, and that of Nazi Germany, would later play a role in many of his works. He served as a radio officer during the war in the Mercantile Marine from 1942 to 1945, and resumed his education afterwards at Durham University, earning his bachelor's degree in 1949. Blackburn taught for several years after that, first in London and then in Berlin, and married Joan Mary Clift in 1950. Returning to London in 1952, he took over the management of Red Lion Books.

It was there that Blackburn began writing, and the immediate success in 1958 of his first novel, *A Scent of New-Mown Hay*, led him to take up a career as a writer full time. He and his wife also maintained an antiquarian bookstore, a secondary career that would inform some of Blackburn's work, including the bibliomystery *Blue Octavo* (1963). *A Scent of New-Mown Hay* typified the approach that would come to characterize Blackburn's twenty-eight novels, which defied easy categorization in their unique and compelling mixture of the genres of science fiction, horror, mystery, and thriller. Many of Blackburn's best novels came in the late 1960s and early 1970s, with a string of successes that included the classics *A Ring of Roses* (1965), *Children of the Night* (1966), *Nothing but the Night* (1968; adapted for a 1973 film starring Christopher Lee and Peter Cushing), *Devil Daddy* (1972) and *Our Lady of Pain* (1974). Somewhat unusually for a popular horror writer, Blackburn's novels were not only successful with the reading public but also won widespread critical acclaim: the *Times Literary Supplement* declared him 'today's master of horror' and compared him with the Grimm Brothers, while the *Penguin Encyclopedia of Horror and the Supernatural* regarded him as 'certainly the best British novelist in his field' and the *St James Guide to Crime & Mystery Writers* called him 'one of England's best practicing novelists in the tradition of the thriller novel'.

By the time Blackburn published his final novel in 1985, much of his work was already out of print, an inexplicable neglect that continued until Valancourt began republishing his novels in 2013. John Blackburn died in 1993.

"We'll hang Jeff Davis on a sour apple tree"
—*John Brown's Body*

CHAPTER ONE

At five o'clock, a man called One walked to the station and the terror began.

Number One was small and neat and pink. He had tiny, pink hands and a pink, bald head and his eyes had little pink flecks in them. At times they didn't seem to focus quite correctly.

All around him, the country town gleamed in sunlight, smelling of summer and the sea. Through a gap at the end of the street he could look back and see the long field of wheat through which he had walked. It had been a good year, and the wheat was very tall, almost up to Number One's shoulder in places. He looked with hatred at those rows of tall wheat.

There were four children playing on the steps to the booking hall, and a yellow dog scratched idly in the sun. Number One kept out of their way. Well in the shade, holding tightly to the side rail, and he carried his precious hate with him as he went. It was the meaning of his life, all he had and all he needed, so he carried it carefully, for it had taken him so long to find. He remembered the thousand sleepless mornings when it had tried to speak to him and always failed. The long walks as a boy, on the heather, and its words had mingled and run with the curlew cries and become meaningless. And then at last it had come. Come silently, confidentially, lifting a flap of bone and creeping into his skull like a small, warm animal. And once there, once established, he knew. Knew with absolute certainty who it was. Knew who had crippled, ruined, cheated him, made him suffer. Knew it was Them. And oh, Dear Lord above, Dear Sweet Jesus, who art in Heaven. God! how he hated them.

But now it was all right. Now the waiting was over and the action lay ahead. Now at last he could repay.

He bought his ticket, squinting with his weak eyes at the clerk behind the slit, and stepped through the barrier. A small, rather appealing figure on the grey waste of the platform.

The big, green engine of the boat express came into the station with a contemptuous rush as though disdaining so mean a halt. Number One walked slowly down the platform and pulled himself up into the last of the first-class coaches. For a time he stood looking out of the window as the train groaned forward and his past slid away from him. Everything was in order, everything was as planned. As he had been told it would be planned. As his hatred had told him. The train was almost empty and the brute would be in a first-class compartment. A smoker probably. They always smoked and they always travelled first class. Rich or poor, they travelled first class. He smiled slightly and began to move forward along the train, peering into each compartment as he went.

It didn't take him long; at the end of the next coach he paused and began to pull at the door handle, bracing himself hard against the lurching of the train. It took all his small strength to pull back the door.

The dark man sat in a corner seat by the window. There were two cases in the rack above him, and he had a paper across his knees. He looked up and smiled as Number One came in. He had a nice smile, and there was a lot of gold in it.

"I wonder, sir—" Number One fought to hold back his stammer. Whatever happened, he mustn't look ridiculous in front of the swine.

"I wonder if you could oblige me with a light?"

The dark man bowed and pushed aside the paper. His smile was like a white and gold beacon as he reached in his pocket. It went out like a beacon too, when he saw what Number One held.

Number One smiled in his turn as he looked at that closed bewildered face, and hate and joy boiled together inside him.

"You bastard," he said softly. "You bloody, dirty bastard." He moved forward into the compartment, and the thing he held looked too heavy for his tiny hand.

Liverpool Street Station in the evening, the lights already orange in the dark, echoing hall and the fog coming down the steps to join the steam, grit and locomotive smoke.

Michael Howard leaned against a pillar, just to the right of the first arrival platform, and he might have been waiting for his girl. Everything about him from his shabby raincoat to his mild, humorous face looked pleasant and slightly academic; he could have been a writer or a lecturer at a provincial university; only his eyes gave him away. They were very cold, very hard eyes and they had seen too much to soften. He was a Foreign Office Intelligence agent, and he had come to hear the end of a story for which his department had waited seventeen years.

All around him, scurrying figures in uniform black and grey jostled their way to the trains, and above his head the loud-speaker burst into hoarse, indistinct life.

"The Six-Five Continental Boat Train is running twelve minutes late. It will now arrive at Platform One, at seventeen minutes past six."

Michael glanced at his watch, looked up at the huge, soot-encrusted clock above his head, and hitching his coat tighter around him, for it was summer in London, moved through the homing crowds to the buffet.

As usual it was packed. He stepped carefully over the piles of knapsacks, suit-cases and umbrellas and finding an empty stool at the bar, ordered a Bass. On the television screen in front of him, the well-fed, reassuring face of Liberace spoke of love and good will to men.

"Extraordinary thing, this business about Barford, sir."

"I beg your pardon. Barford?" Michael turned politely to the man with the paper beside him.

"Yes, Barford, the Wakefield hatchet murderer. The police got him this morning in a public convenience; in Staines of all places." He drank deeply from his pint glass, put a cigarette to his lips and leaned confidentially over towards Michael.

"Makes you think, doesn't it? Two years and three months ago this chap cuts his wife to pieces in Yorkshire. He clears out, leaving the body in the house, and seems to disappear completely. For over two years he goes free. Must have begun to think he was in the clear by now, I shouldn't wonder; then somebody spots him and they pick him up in a Gents. You know, I reckon that once those boys get their hooks into you, you might as well give up. Blimey, two ruddy years."

"Yes, I'm sure you're right, two years, a long time." Michael turned away from him, and thought of the man for whom they had waited fifteen years. The man who had done the worst thing in the world and then vanished completely. The man they wanted more than anyone else on their files. He, and the other man. The one who after all those years had claimed to know something. The man who had rung the department, getting the number by some unknown, tortuous method, and arranged this meeting. The man who by now was almost home. Lurching home towards him through the eastern suburbs in his corner seat, with nothing about him that mattered, except this one promise of information which might close a file.

Outside the Tannoy burst into life, drowning the notes of the tenor on the screen.

"The Six-Five Boat Train from Harwich is now approaching Platform One."

Michael drained his glass; dust on his skin, and sediment on his tongue, and nodding affably to his bar companion moved out to the hall.

As he had expected, the train was half empty. He stood back from the platform edge, and watched the procession of ruck-sacked Germans, weary businessmen and hard-faced army wives as they streeled past him to the barrier; and amongst them there was no one he wanted. No broad, dark-faced figure clutching a brief-case hurried towards him. No one at all. After a moment his attitude changed. He became a harassed passenger who had left hat or gloves behind and hurried forward to the train, pausing for a moment as two girls, chattering like hoarse sparrows, stepped past him. Then he climbed up the steps into the corridor.

The girls had been almost the last to leave. Almost, but not quite. He was nearly to the end of the train, when he paused and gently pulled back the door.

The man he had come to meet sat very still in the corner with his back to the engine. There was a newspaper on the seat beside him and he held a cigarette lighter in his hand. He seemed to smile with his eyes at Michael. His eyes were very deep, very dark and liquid, and he had three of them. Two were rather wide set in his broad, handsome face and the other was almost in the centre of his forehead.

He did not appear to have bled a great deal.

CHAPTER TWO

Under the torn hand, across the table, over the enormous, multi-coloured map, the long trains of Europe came home.

"Friday," said the voice above the map. "Just last Friday this chap Vanek manages to get our number and phones us. I show mild and hesitant interest in the information he promises, and though I don't really believe he is on to anything, arrange a meeting. After that, Friend Vanek springs into activity. He applies for a week's leave of absence from the North Country Hospital, where he works, and takes a continental holiday. We know from his passport that he visited Holland and Germany, returning here last night for his appointment with you. Like a good chap, he didn't keep you waiting."

General Charles Kirk, Head of Her Majesty's Foreign Office Intelligence in Europe, pulled himself up from the desk and crossed the room to the huge electric fire that stood in the corner. For a long moment he bent in front of it, slowly massaging his left hand that lacked three fingers before the bars, then he turned and looked at Michael Howard. His heavy, well-bred features were very tired and completely without expression.

"Well, Mike," he said. "And where do we go from here?"

Michael didn't answer him for a moment. He ground his cigarette out in the already overflowing ashtray and he didn't seem to think about anything at all.

"Tell me, sir," he said at last. "Let's forget Vanek for a moment. Tell me about Glyde. What was he really like?"

Kirk left the fire and took a heavy buff folder from a filing cabinet. He threw it on the desk over the map.

"It's a long time," he said slowly. "A long, long time ago, eighteen years to be exact, and I only saw him for perhaps half an hour when he came here for his security check with the Ministry, you know the details of that. I haven't a clue what he was like, but I can tell you one thing, Mike, at the time I think I liked him. Yes, I think so. He had a strange quality which was surprisingly attractive. It wasn't like being with a human being at all, but rather as if he was some kind of machine and the only thing that kept it going was one's own approval. It was uncanny but somehow rather flattering and pleasant. Yes, John Glyde was quite certainly the worst human creature I have ever come in contact with, and I think I liked him."

He broke off and pushed the folder across the desk to Michael.

"Take a look at him, Boy. It's all there, every stage of his life, as far as we know it. It's been almost a personal hobby of mine, a private scrap-album of the Devil."

The book was a mass of pictures, and beside each picture there was a date and notes in Kirk's sprawling hand. The first photograph had been crudely tinted in colour. It showed a child standing on a lawn before a Georgian house. He was wearing a sailor suit with very wide bell-bottoms and H.M.S. Lion was written on his cap. His eyes were a very pale blue and he held a Dutch doll in his hands. The doll had no eyes; they had been removed.

Michael turned over the pages and the child started to grow. The sailor suits gave way to Eton collars and football jerseys, the school groups changed to young men and women in punts and sports cars. It all altered except one thing. The expression on the boy's face never changed, but remained quite constant. It was an expression of cunning, sham hope and a sublime indifference to anything outside itself, as if the Buddha had somehow merged with a race-course tipster. Michael turned on to the last page and suddenly everything stopped. The sports cars drove away, the Oxford bags faded, the girls in summer dresses went home. In the final picture only the boy was left, sitting there quite alone in a uniform that had never seen Sandhurst.

"Yes, I see what you mean." Michael closed the folder and pushed it away from him. "And nobody had any suspicion of his leanings till he went over?"

"Not a soul. I don't even know that he had any leanings, I feel it may have been mere perversity on his part. He was pretty good at his job, and the Ministry sent him over to Paris in the early part of 1940. He was a sort of liaison officer to the French Information Bureau. When the German advance got close to the city, he was told to get out as best as he could with the other people. He is known to have packed his bags and then went off, saying he wanted to say goodbye to someone, and would be at the fixed rendezvous an hour later. He never turned up and they went without him. You know the rest."

Michael did know the rest. He watched his chief lean back and put a match to his cold cigar. The grey wisps of smoke spiralled upwards to nothing, like the trail of the lost years, and he thought of the man Kirk had passed at the security check. The official in an obscure government department whom they had sent to France and who disappeared amid the ruin of the retreating armies. Disappeared completely, until a year later, when he had come back. Come back when the Blitz was orange in the streets, the smoke all around like fog and the night loud with the sirens of the rescue teams; while on the radio came a calm, level and utterly reasonable voice.

"This is John Glyde speaking to you from Germany."

"Yes," said Kirk, "and I liked him. I think it was the implication he gave that your interest and approval was the one thing that mattered to him. That was probably what made him so effective on the radio. The others were just punks. Joyce, Baillie Stewart, Amery. We laughed at them, and because we laughed they were worth divisions to us. But not him. We didn't laugh at John Glyde, we didn't laugh one little bit. Can you still remember any of those broadcasts, Mike? This one for instance. 'I want to speak to the wife of Serjeant Robin Napier of Preston, whose husband has just lost both his legs.' The bastard, the bloody, dirty, treacherous bastard." For a moment, Kirk's hand drummed quickly on the desk.

"And it wasn't just what he did on the radio. Oh no, not just that. There were the other things, the things that happened in the camps. Yes, Mike, treason is one thing, killing another. Both bad perhaps, but I think there are worse. The deliberate destruction of a soul, for example. The use of every force, physical, moral, sexual for just that end, and always on the young. Stoker Roach, sixteen, Davies, eighteen, Kent, twenty. All traitors, all made by Glyde.

"Do you know what my victory dream was, Boy? Not the dream of peace, not the slackening of fear, not getting tight and waving a flag with the Americans in Piccadilly Circus. Not anything like that. Just one tiny, little, unimportant thing. The punishment of that man."

"Yes, sir, I understand, but it seems the Germans might have forestalled you."

"Yes, it seems like that. Glyde made his last broadcast from Hamburg on August the tenth, 1944. His final visit to Stalag Thirteen was a couple of days earlier. After the tenth, he disappeared, just vanished completely. As soon as the war finished, as you know, I went to Germany and tried to look for him. And what did I find, not a trace. It was as if he had been swallowed up. All notes, every file on him had been destroyed on the orders of Himmler himself. One of his colleagues at the radio station was executed for merely mentioning his name. It almost seemed that even to the worst of the Nazis he had become something too evil to talk about.

"Well, as I told you, after a few interrogations, I became sure that Glyde was dead, probably liquidated. I closed our office files and I just kept this." He grinned at the folder in front of him.

"Until last week."

"Yes, until last week. Last Friday a man rings me up. A man of no importance. An obscure Czech refugee who is at present working as a male nurse in a mental hospital. He tells me he has some information for sale about Glyde. He tells me that he believes Glyde may still be alive. He arranges a meeting for yesterday because he says he needs time to get full confirmation of what he thinks. Well, we don't know if he got it. All we know is that he got something. He got enough to earn him a thirty-two bullet slap through the middle of his frontal lobe."

He paused as the phone rang and motioned Michael to take it.

"Hullo, this is Room 24. Yes, Michael Howard speaking." He spoke almost indifferently and then tensed.

"Yes, Superintendent. What! Hang on a minute." His hand scrabbled for pencil and paper. "Right, go on. The Devil you say. Yes, I see. Yes, I've got it, but it sounds incredible. And you're sure, you're quite sure. I don't know what to make of it, but you'll get in touch when you have more detail. Very well, thanks for ringing. Yes, thanks, Super." He dropped the phone back on to its rest and looked at Kirk. There was a look of complete bewilderment on his face.

"A nut," he said, "a ruddy nut killed Vanek. A chap called Thoday, definitely unbalanced, been in and out of mental homes for years. No doubt about it, sir, the gun and the prints check. He was still holding the gun. They found him on the line ten miles south of Colchester. He killed Vanek all right and when he'd done that he really went to town with himself. Chucked himself out of a window of the train and then, for good measure, put a bullet through his head as he fell."

"So that's that. A psychopath, eh, with no rational reason for his actions." Kirk pulled himself out of his seat and looked down at the grey stream of Whitehall.

"And that finishes it. When Vanek first spoke to me I thought he was just a crank trying to draw attention to himself. I felt he had heard about the Glyde story and was using it for his own advertisement. Nothing more. When he was killed I began to believe he was on to something. Now, I suppose, we can pack up again. His killer was one of the insane. I'm not justified in wasting public money on Vanek: it's up to the police." He stood quite motionless for a minute and suddenly his face changed.

"No, by God, it's not."

He turned away from the window, and walking back into the room, pulled open a drawer of his heavy, old-fashioned filing cabinet.

"Come here, Mike, and take these." He handed him a thick wad of indexed cards.

"No, I don't give a damn if I am wasting public money. I want to know the truth, so I'm going after the story of Vanek and the story of this man Thoday as if everything I was told was the literal truth and Vanek did know something about Glyde.

"We're going in, Mike. We're going to check on Thoday and Vanek and everybody who was even remotely connected with the Glyde story, and we're going to tear them right apart. We're also going to interest ourselves in the study of mental health. We're going to be very careful about that part. Very careful indeed. I've got an idea that we're up against something very different from our usual jobs and we're going to go easy. I don't like people who kill and then throw themselves out of trains. So we're going to take things very steady. As I look at it, there have been two too many bodies already.

"Now, take these and prepare a visiting list. All Glyde's contacts that you can find. The parents are dead. But I think there may be a sister. Yes, there should still be a sister." His voice was very thoughtful as he said that.

When Michael had left him, Kirk went back to his desk and once more bent over the album. Again the child with the blind doll looked up at him.

"Well, Pet," he said, and his voice was very gentle. "We all thought you were dead, didn't we? 'Cold in the earth and fifteen wild Decembers,' eh, John. Well, you may be dead or you may not. And if not, if you're alive and anywhere on this planet, then I'm going to get you."

For quite a long time he stared at the photograph. His cigar smoke swirled round the stifling room, the red electric clock on the wall ran on. Outside it was bright morning. Exactly twelve hours had passed since the train had left Harwich.

CHAPTER THREE

On the morning that they sold the Lancia, Penny Wise got out of bed and knew that things were on the up and up.

There was nothing at all to account for it. At first glance it was just the same as any other morning. The bedroom looked as untidy as ever. On the side table there was the usual glass and the overflowing ashtray. Her mouth still tasted slightly of gin and tonic. It was the regular start to the day.

But there was something different about it. Something exciting, and evanescent as spring, was in the air. The sun lapped mottled through the leaves over the mews. There was a smell of coffee from the next door flat, and below in the garage, she could hear her partner Tony Field whistling "Abide with Me," as he faked up the Ford's back axle.

"Hey ding-a ding-a ding," sang Penny untunefully as she pulled on the slippers and walked to the bathroom.

She was a fine, big girl with a lot of blond hair that looked dyed but wasn't. She wore her own teeth and breasts, and she was just young enough to be able to tell her age. She had been christened Penelope, but with her surname everybody called her Penny; she was that kind of girl.

She washed leisurely and with pleasure and then, making some coffee in the tiny kitchen, went through into the sitting-room, where her clothes of last night were draped over the back of an arm-chair. She eyed them with distaste, and taking her coffee to a desk by the window, picked up a stiff-backed exercise book.

The book was neatly divided into columns, giving names, dates and times with a few pencilled notes below each. They all concerned forthcoming transactions. A methodical and business-like firm were "Messrs. Wise Motors." That morning there was only one entry that concerned her. A note on the top of the page. "Thornton, 10. Method 2." She glanced at the clock over the man-telpiece. Yes, dead on ten now. He'd be along any minute. Still, she had plenty of time; say ten minutes pep talk with Tony and then ten round the block. There was no need to hurry, and she had to look just right for Method 2. The dark serge again, she sup-posed. It had been good once, and now, well worn, gave just the right hint of genteel poverty. Hair back in a band. Pale make-up on the face, with a hint, a very slight suspicion of lipstick. "Better days, old girl, better days. Poverty, hunger and dirt," said Penny Wise, and moved to the window as the footsteps sounded in the yard.

The man didn't just walk into the mews, he strutted. He was on a stage and the World was his audience. Head back, shoulders braced, cane, with its silver knob, clicking exactly in time with his polished right shoe, he was a fine sight. Not very big perhaps, not at all big, but he made up for it. Blue blazer with crest and motto, stiff cap, cuffs and gloves, bow tie with the little gold flecks in it, pipe clutched manfully in his strong white dentures, he made a dashing picture. He had almost everything he needed to get through life. Penny felt inclined to clap as he rounded the bend of the yard and saw Tony come out of the garage to greet him. Yes, very much Method 2.

"Ah, Mr. Thornton, here you are, sir, dead on time." Tony Field's manner had just the right mixture of deference and affability. He'd put a lot of work into it. It was for this reason he called himself Captain, though actually he had once risen to the rank of Major.

"Never does to have a higher rank than your average customer," he had told Penny. "Besides, isn't there something rather dashing about Captain? Something heroic and biblical, 'Captain of Thousands.' "

"Yes, darling," she had replied coldly. "Something rather dishonest as well. Why is it that when somebody tries to play a confidence trick he so often calls himself Captain?"

Now Tony stood before Thornton and smiled ruefully at his stained overalls. There was something very attractive and boyish about his smile. He had spent hours in front of a mirror getting it just right.

"Awfully sorry to have to receive you like this," he said. "Fact is, trade's been so bad lately, I just don't seem able to afford a proper staff."

"Don't give it a thought, old boy, I quite understand." Thornton enjoyed magnanimity towards the less successful.

"Good of you to write to me. Sorry I couldn't get over before, but—Business." His white hand waved in a circle to describe the vastness of his affairs.

"Quite so. Well, now you're here, come and take a look at her. I've put her round the corner all ready for you. Nice job, think you'll like her, hope you will." He leaned confidentially over.

"Fact is, I spent a packet too much on her. Must try and get some of it back. Also, while we've had her here, Mrs. Wise has been driving her." He lowered his voice. "I don't like it, you know. Good enough driver in her way, as some women are, but this is a fast motor-car. When she gets a home, I want it to be with someone who can really handle her. That's why I thought of you." Thornton nodded gravely at the compliment.

The Lancia stood at the end of the mews, and she was very long, very red and very beautiful. She had a special body and a high compression engine. It had taken a lot of love and a lot of money to make her. That was a long time ago, for now she was old; and like every sports car she had lived too well. She was like an ageing, gay lady who had taken too many stock-brokers, and too many undergraduates to her bed. She had been driven too fast and too far, for too long. There had been too many roadhouses, too many trips to Brighton, too many spins on the Continent. She was burned out and only Thornton's ego could possibly save her.

He walked slowly round her, pulling and pushing at gadgets, fiddling with the bodywork and he saw nothing at all that mattered.

"Yes, quite a girl, isn't she?" Tony's voice was both sad and loving. "Wherever you parked, wherever you took her you need never be ashamed of her. Yes, quite a girl. I hate the word, sir, but she's—well—a gentleman's car."

"Quite, I know what you mean." Thornton looked keenly at him. "Well, mind if I take her round the block for a while?"

"Go ahead." Tony held the door open for him. "You know where everything is, don't you? Go easy with her though, she's very fast. You'll forgive my not coming with you, won't you? You'll get a better idea on your own, and I've got so much to do."

He stood back as Thornton jerked the car forward, grinding his gears and mercilessly over-revving the engine.

"Silly sod," he thought. "Hope to hear some loose bearings, do you? Not with that axle oil in the sump. Not this time, Old Top."

He only had ten minutes to wait. He bent over the Ford with the broken crown wheel, and he didn't straighten at once when Thornton roared to a stop beside him.

"Well," he said. "Wasn't I right about her, sir?"

"Yes, in a way, but I'm not quite sure." The Lancia was just what Thornton needed to complete his ego, but she was a lot of money. "She didn't seem to have so many guts, you know."

"Oh, that." Tony smiled indulgently. "You must remember she's an Italian, and that she was cold. What was it old Alfredo Bugatti said to Bentley?" He racked his brains for something Alfredo Bugatti might have said in one of his weaker moments. "Yes, they never walk unless they boil, Mr. Bentley. Wasn't that it?"

"Yes, something like that, I seem to remember. Still, you're asking a lot of money for her."

"Don't I know it. All the same, I could probably sell her to some rich know-nothing for well above the list price even now. I don't want to do that if I can help it, though. I'd like her to have a good home, to go to someone who appreciate good things. Somebody who loves fine cars, and at the same time won't miss the odd hundred or so. That's why I thought of you, of course."

"Quite so," Thornton seemed to swell a little with his words, but he was still undecided. "Tell you what, I'll sleep on it and let you know tomorrow."

Tony glanced up at the flat window and winked his eye at his last card. The one queen of trumps which could still win the rubber. She didn't disappoint him.

"Tony, what are you doing with my car?" Her accent was just right. Annoyance, anxiety, and a hint of pound notes that had blown away. Her clothes were right too. The faded costume that had cost a lot of money, a long time ago. The low-heeled, hand-sewn shoes that had seen much mileage. Even the thin make-up and the haunted, anxious eyes were exactly in keeping.

"Tony," she said. "You're not—you're not trying to sell my car, are you? I know things are bad, but surely not as bad as that. She's the one lovely thing I've still got left." Her fingers ran softly along the steep, rectangular bonnet, and suddenly, for the first time, she seemed to see Thornton.

"Oh, I'm sorry, so terribly sorry. I'm afraid I was upset, I didn't see you for a moment. You're not going to buy her, are you? I'm sure you're the kind of person who would look after her, but I do so hate the thought of parting with her." There was water in the blue eyes now.

"Sorry, Mr. Thornton, bit of a crisis, I'm afraid. Excuse us a moment."

Tony laid his arm on Penny's shoulder, and led her to the door, talking as he went.

"Look, I know it's your car. I know it's a wonderful job. I know I'm asking too little for it, but try and see reason. Just remember what that devil at the bank said when I rang him last week, and you'll see there's nothing else we can do."

His stage whisper rang round the yard like a full orchestra, and as he listened, Thornton began to see the true value of the Lancia. He fingered the cheque book in his breast pocket, looked greedily at the red car, and decided.

Penny took off the dark costume and threw it on the bed. She wiped her face carefully and painted her lips a bright scarlet. Finally she pulled on a gold blouse and a pair of jeans. She felt much better like that.

"Well, partner, we made it." Tony stood in the doorway, and there was a slip of paper in his hand.

"Of course we did. Never any doubt about it, once I brought on the agony act. How much did you get for the old heap anyway? She took the cheque out of his hand and gazed at it fondly.

"Yerse, not bad. Not bad at all, ducks. Exactly what we had in mind as the very top figure. Let me see. That should give us a profit of—she pursed her lips in thought—"yes, a profit of very nearly two hundred and ten per cent.

"Aren't I brilliant, Tony? I wonder what this miserable concern would do without me."

"Do very well, not so many overheads for one thing." He glanced at the open doors of the wardrobe. "Well, honey, some of us have got to do some work. I must have that Ford axle fixed by lunch, so it's quite literally back to the grindstone."

When he had gone, Penny locked the cheque carefully up in the desk, and set about repairing the ravages to the flat. She worked slowly and without enthusiasm, for she hated house-work, and glad of any break in her duties, turned quickly to the door as the bell rang.

The man at the door didn't look as if he had come to buy or sell. He was too unpushing for one thing and there was some-thing very cynical about his mild face. He took off his hat, and gave her a polite good-morning and a card.

"Mr. Howard." Penny glanced at the card and then looked at him. "Now what are you, a prospective vendor or purchaser? Let me think. Frankly you don't look like either. You look quite respectable. I wonder what you want."

"Thank you, Mrs. Wise. Very nice of you." Michael grinned at her. "I'm afraid I've got a car and I don't want to sell it just yet. Actually I wanted to have a word with you, if I may."

"But of course you may. I am most flattered. You'd better come up and tell me what it is all about."

She led the way upstairs to the flat, and switching off a screaming vacuum cleaner, motioned him to the sofa.

"Sorry about this dump. With the great pressure of business I haven't been able to clear up yet." She glanced at the clock, and moved across to a cupboard. "Eleven o'clock. They're open. What would you like? I've got gin or whiskey."

"Scotch, please, lot of water." Michael looked hard at her as she poured the drinks. Under the flippant exterior, there was something else in her face. An expression which she was desperately trying to conceal.

"Well, Mr. Howard, not a salesman of anything, I think. No, quite definitely not a salesman. Not nearly smart enough for one thing, and you lack the jolly air of friendly helpfulness. I don't want to be over-curious or pushing, but I wonder just what you do want." She sipped her gin, and looked at him from under her long eyelashes. They were just short enough to be possibly real.

Michael didn't answer her for a moment. This was just the kind of business he hated. He took a long pull at his whiskey before he spoke and when he did, his voice was very gentle.

"Mrs. Wise, I understand that you were married in July, 1951. Before that you had changed your name to Bryant by deed of poll. Before these two changes, your family name was Glyde. That's what I want to talk to you about."

He turned away his face and waited for the storm. The storm and the reproaches and the tears; they did not come. Very calmly, she put down the glass she was holding and smiled at him.

"Good," she said. "Almost very good. The nice, honest, direct, straight from the shoulder, manly approach. Usually they put it in writing, but I much prefer your way. Well, Mr. Howard, I didn't think it was still news, but, how much?"

"Sorry, I'm not with you. How much for what?"

"How much for the story, the interview, of course. It may be old stuff, but it's still worth more than a light. Should go down well in your 'World's Odd Tales' or something. After all, treason, a vanishing trick, two suicides thrown in. I feel your editor should still pay pretty well, you know."

"I see, I'm sorry, but I'm afraid you're on the wrong track. All my fault, I should have told you before." He put his hand deep in his back pocket, past the fish-hook that was sewn there, and gave her the embossed slip of his official pass.

For a moment, she looked quite incuriously at it, and then her expression changed. The features didn't alter, but behind the features, she became hard, and frightened, and very much alone. She picked up her glass and moved back to the cupboard with it. It was almost neat gin she used this time.

"So, that's who you are, Mr. Howard. 'Home is the sailor, home from the sea, and the Hunter home from the hill.' Seventeen years have passed. My parents are dead, John is said to be dead, a lot of me has died too, yet you still come. You still come and ask questions, don't you? No, not you. Not you, Mr. Howard; you're all wrong. You look wrong. I know exactly what you should be like. You should be stout and middle-aged, and have a Scottish accent and a fatherly manner. You shouldn't sit down, and you shouldn't accept a drink. The proper thing is to stand in the centre of the room, and twist a bowler hat in your hands. Shall I show you? It might help you to advance in your disagreeable profession."

She came across, and stood in front of him, and so good was her mimicry, that for a moment she disappeared and the man she had described took her place.

"Ah'm verra, verra sorry to hev to distarb ye once more, Miss," said Inspector McAlpine of Special Branch. "Please dinna be alermed, as this is a purely routine enquiry. I hev to ask ye however hif ye may have received any communication pertaining to yer bruther, at any time, since his dissaperence."—As though checked in flight, McAlpine's words were cut short, and his bowler described circles as he waved something aside.

"Ah, noo, thank ee, Marm. Partial as Ah hem to a glass, not on duty. Well, got the idea." It came as a shock as her own voice switched to normal.

"Many thanks," said Michael. "I see what you mean, next time I'll try and do better."

For a moment, a terrible desire came over him. He wanted to get up from the sofa and go out. Go out, and take this girl with him. Take her away from their memories. Away from the traitor who had vanished, the three-eyed thing in the train, the dead madman. Out in a fast car, through the morning suburbs to the long hills of the West, with only the whine of the tyres in his ears and her hair on his shoulder. He forced himself back to duty, but desire was still very strong in him.

"Yes, next time, I'll try and do better, but not now. You see, my dear, this isn't routine. The fact is that yesterday we received a piece of information which makes us think your brother may, just possibly, be still alive."

And that hit her. It hit her hard. She seemed to sway as with a physical blow, and the glass tilted in her hand, sending a stream of clear liquid over his hat on the table. But even as she swayed, Michael saw something in her face that was not shock. It wasn't anything describable, but it was not shock, it was not surprise, and it was only there for a second. Then her own face came together again.

"Sorry," she said. "Terribly sorry, I've ruined your hat, though it's a dreadful hat, isn't it?"

She picked it up and slowly brushed it dry with her hand. Then she sat down beside him.

"So you think John may be alive, may I ask you why?"

And Michael told her. He broke the most sacred rule in the department and told her exactly what they knew, and as he talked he saw certainty grow in her face.

"Yes, I think your Mr. Vanek may just possibly have been right. I've no facts to support my idea, but I think he may have been right.

"You see, if you'd ever met John, you'd know that he wasn't the kind of person to just go and die. I don't think he was like a person at all, as we use the word. He was more like a mass of atmosphere, a presence. And you know, Mr. Howard, I don't believe you can kill just a presence." She leaned back and smiled again at Michael.

"Sorry, I'm afraid that sounds a lot of nonsense, I'll try and explain.

"John was eleven years older than I. I was just twelve when he went to France but I can still remember him very well. You see, Mr. Howard, I think I may have loved him. Oh, no, not love in any adoring adolescent way, but rather as if I belonged to him. John had one very endearing quality. When you were with him he made you feel that in the whole world you were the only person who mattered to him. It was very attractive, almost like a form of possession in a way.

"It happened to my parents as well I think. That's why the end was so very much the end for them." She still smiled at Michael, but there was a terrible emptiness behind her eyes.

"No, I don't think he would die. My father died, my mother died, and I'm half dead from the waist up, but I don't think John died.

"What is your first name, Mr. Howard? Michael. Michael Howard. A nice name. Nice, strong, kind Michael Howard. Oh, yes, you've been very kind and I don't suppose you've ever done anything not very sensible in your whole life, have you, Michael? That's why you'll never understand the John Glydes of this world. People like you; decent, sane, sensible people, never can know people like him. The fey ones, the empty ones. The ones who aren't really like proper people at all. The ones whose actions don't seem real or personal but are just—"

She broke off with a jerk and pulled a cigarette from a crumpled packet on the table. Michael leaned forward and lit it for her.

"No, I'm sorry, but I think I do understand just a little." As she had been speaking he had remembered Kirk's words. 'Just a machine which needed your approval to keep it going.' "Yes," he said, "I do understand what you mean."

"Do you, Michael? Do you understand? Yes, perhaps you do, just a little. Let me go on." Her fingers drew lightly along his sleeve as she spoke.

"Try and imagine an autumn night, a long time ago. It was my birthday as it happened, September the fourth. You might remember that date. My mother had put herself out for that birthday. She'd baked a cake and even got hold of a few candles. It was a very special effort in wartime. I was off to boarding school in the morning. As you doubtless know, I didn't go, but we thought so at the time, and it was like a parting of the ways.

"Well, there were no other guests, the Blitz was still active, but we enjoyed ourselves, I think. Just my father who had got back early from the Ministry, my mother and I. We were worried about John of course, but as you know there had been very little actual fighting in the Paris area, and we'd been told he was probably a prisoner and that we'd hear in time. I can remember pulling crackers and laughing a lot, and blowing out the candles. There weren't thirteen, I'm afraid, but they looked nice. Well, that was all. We ate the cake, and as a special treat: my parents weren't Puritans, whatever the papers said, they gave me a glass of sherry.

"At nine o'clock, my father turned on the news. I can remember it almost word for word. Hull had been blitzed the night before. A destroyer had been sunk by a mine in the Channel. The R.A.F. had made a daylight raid on Wilhelmshaven.

"That was that: now comes the interesting part. After my father had turned off the set, we sat back and looked at the fire. We must have been like that for perhaps ten minutes and then I got a terrible feeling that somebody wanted to speak to us. I looked across at my mother and from her expression I knew that she was feeling the same. She nodded suddenly and at the same moment I heard my father's voice. 'Penny, please turn on the wireless to Lord Haw Haw.'

"Well, then it came. In all I suppose it must have lasted about a quarter of an hour. I knew straight away that it was him, before he even gave his name; and you know, Michael, all the time he was speaking I didn't care. I didn't care a damn what he'd done. I didn't mind that he was a traitor. I just listened to his voice and I—yes, I loved him.

"As soon as he'd finished my father got up and switched off the set. 'Go up to bed now, Penny,' he said. 'That wasn't John, it was just a lie, just faked propaganda. You mustn't pay any attention to it at all. Go on now. Doris and Mary will look after you.' We still ran to a couple of maids in those days.

"Well, Michael, Mickey, Mike, whichever you prefer, that's the lot, all I know. You should be able to guess the rest."

And he didn't need to guess the rest, he knew. He saw the girl with blonde plats who was going to school in the morning listening to the voice of the traitor and still loving him. He saw the half-eaten cake and the cold candles; the less than thirteen cold candles. He saw the Under Secretary, due for a knighthood, who had come home early, still anxious about his son, but determined to keep his daughter's birthday. He saw that man listening to the radio, and as he listened, thinking. Thinking "he can't. He can't have done this thing. He couldn't have done it." Then at last would come the final conclusion, the last whisper of despair. "But by God! he has."

The rest was easy to imagine. The face of cowardice looking at him. The child sent to bed. The walk to the door, with his hand trembling on his wife's. The waiting car. The bombs and the blackout. The sudden mad acceleration towards the embankment and the Thames mud.

"Yes," he said. "Perhaps I can guess the rest."

"Perhaps you can, Mike." He could feel her hand very tight and warm on his arm now. "Perhaps you can, but whatever you do, don't start pitying me. There's nothing about me that needs pity. I got over it. Alive or dead, John has gone out of my life. I married a fool as soon as I found one foolish enough to take me, and though he left me when he knew who I was, I'm all right. I run a good business here which keeps me and my partner and my partner's wife and half a dozen hangers-on in moderate comfort. I'm hard and cold and quite efficient, so don't worry about me. Just worry about John, because if he is alive you may have plenty to worry about. And remember what I said. He wasn't like a person. He was just a mass of atmosphere, a presence. A presence that at times could get so near to you that it could almost make you think its thoughts. I know something about that. Perhaps it is a family tendency, because at times I feel I have it too, slightly." She leaned back against the cushions and looked at him. There was an expression in her eyes that had not been there before.

"Haven't I got it a little, Mike? Haven't I? Just try and tell me what I'm thinking about now, Mike."

Michael Howard looked at her and suddenly he knew what he had to do. Against every rule of conduct, sense and duty, he knew what he had to do. Knew, like an order what he should, had, ought to do. All at once the glass was out of his hand, and his arm was around her; while very gently, very firmly and softly, like something coming home, his other hand reached for her zipper.

"Hullo, Penny Wise," said Pound Foolish.

CHAPTER FOUR

It could have been any canteen or snack-bar anywhere. It had the familiar plastic trays, the same racks of plates, the same bright urns, the same patient queue at the counter.

Kirk moved behind his host between the tables, and looked with interest at the waiting groups. On the surface he could see nothing different about them. They were of every age group, and every physical type. They could have been typical of any crowd in any street, just as long as you didn't know. As long as you didn't look too hard into any one face and make out the something else behind it.

Dr. Grace led him through the restaurant and turned off into a long, white corridor. He shouted as he went, and his legs thudded like pistons on the composition floor. At the end of the passage he threw open a door, and raising a hand like a flipper, half waved and half pushed Kirk forward into a room that smelt strongly of leather arm-chairs, pipe smoke and books. He hurled a pile of papers from a chair by the table and pulled it back.

"Take a pew, General," he boomed, and crossing to a corner cupboard pulled out a bottle and two glasses.

"Excuse the mess, won't you? Never manage to get things properly straight. It's good of you to have come down personally. Very good. I appreciate it. Always like to talk to the man at the top, when necessary. Pity about poor Vanek of course, great pity. Especially as it was an ex-patient of ours who did it. Makes me feel slightly responsible. Say when." His huge hand grasped the bottle like a weapon.

"Thank you. When! When!" Kirk's voice rose slightly as the amber liquid gushed forth as from a tap.

"Right, a little splash. Good." The doctor squirted the merest suspicion of soda into the glasses and carried them to the table.

"I knew you'd drink whiskey, you know. Part of my job to sense things like that." The chair groaned violently as he lowered his bulk into it.

"Well, General, shall we get down to it?" He took a blackened pipe from his pocket and lit it with care before going on.

"Just how can I help you? It's certainly a most unfortunate business, but I've told the Inspector feller all I know, I think. Now you come on the scene. Foreign Office Intelligence, eh. Most exciting, I've always wanted to have a yarn with one of your chaps, but just exactly where do you fit into this business?"

Kirk lit a cigar before replying. "Sorry, Doctor," he said. "I'm afraid I can't tell you where I do come in. Please don't misunderstand me. It isn't that I want to be secretive about anything. It's just that at the moment I don't know myself." He leaned back and watched the wisps of smoke float upwards.

"You see, Doctor, I have to find out about Stephen Vanek. Who was he? That's what seems to be important. We know the bones of his life, of course. We know he was a Czech refugee who came to this country via France and served in the Air Force. We know that after the war he spent most of his life drifting from one job to another. Chef in a café one year, hall porter the next. Always that kind of thing. Quite respectable in his way. The police have no record of dishonesty on his part. Just slightly shiftless.

"A little over six months ago, he applies for a position with you as a Ward Orderly. He has had no previous experience of the job, but because the labour market is tight, you engage him. You are quite satisfied with his work and want to keep him, so that when he applies for a week's leave of absence, for personal reasons, you grant it at once. That was eight days ago.

"What happened in those eight days is this. Vanek went to a post office where he kept his savings and drew out everything he had. One hundred and twelve pounds, to be exact. After that he took the evening boat to the Hook of Holland. We know that he was four days in Germany and visited Berlin.

"Last Monday he returned to England and was found dead, in a first class compartment of the Harwich boat train. His killer is known to be a man called Peter Thoday, who committed suicide shortly after he killed Vanek. Thoday had once been a patient at this hospital. All this, of course, will have been told you by the police, and is not rightly my affair. All I want is one thing. I want to know Thoday's motive, and at the moment I'm not concerned with anything else, I just want to know why he killed him.

"You see, shortly before Vanek asked you for his leave, he rang up my department and offered to sell us a piece of information. He would give no details, but said that if we were interested, he would have to get more facts and would talk to us when he got back from the Continent. Well, I arranged a meeting. My assistant went to Liverpool Street to hear what he had to say, and found him, dead. That's the story so far."

He reached out and flicked his match into an ashtray. It was shaped like a cricket ball and there was a dedication on the base.

"Like you, Doctor, I've got to listen to a lot of people in my job. At the beginning, I never believed Vanek. I thought he was probably an exhibitionist, who had got hold of an old story, and wanted to draw attention to himself with it. When he was killed, I began to think he might have known something. I felt he had been murdered to stop him telling that something. Now we know his killer was probably insane and there might be no motive at all for his action, or possibly a quite illogical one. That's what I want to ask you, Doctor. Peter Thoday was here. You must have known his case. Can you imagine any motive that he may have had?"

Grace didn't reply at once. He got up and looked out of the window at the long slope of the hospital grounds, as they ran down the hill to join the dark suburbs of Tynecastle. In the far distance he could see a trail of smoke, as a train plumed its way to the south.

"Before I try and answer that, General Kirk, can you tell me what was the information Vanek promised you?"

"Sorry, Doctor, I'm afraid not at the moment. I'd like to, but it's quite impossible."

"Very well, then. Let me think." As he watched him, Kirk saw Mr. Pickwick leave his face and it became very fine drawn and scholarly.

"Yes, Thoday would have had a motive." He walked back to the table and slowly drained his glass.

"You see, General Kirk, to the layman the insane are always thought to be illogical. That is why there is terror felt about insanity. But, I am sorry to say, that the idea of the pathological killer attacking without logical reason is a complete fallacy." He put down his glass on the table and leaned against the mantelpiece. On the wall above his head there were a pair of rowing sculls; they had Clare 27 painted in black over the amber varnish.

"Yes, the mentally sick are always perfectly logical. Perhaps that is why they are sick, in a way. In certain cases, some pressure from the past produces a fear, an antipathy, a hatred, which builds itself up until the only chance of the patient's survival seems to him to lie in its removal. Hence the perfectly logical violence which is sometimes found. In this case, what is important, is that it is selective. The fear, the hatred is selective. You have no wish or need to destroy everything, but just the one thing or group of things which seems to threaten you. Bishops, perhaps, men with red hair, foreigners, rubber rain coats, prostitutes. What we've got to find, General, is what Thoday's particular *bête noir* may have been. If we can do that, then I'll be a long way towards answering your question."

He pressed the switch of an old type intercom on the wall and spoke into it before going on.

"I didn't deal with Thoday myself, General, so I've sent for the specialist who did. I can't promise, of course, because the treatment was never finished, but she might be able to tell you something."

"So you think that this was just a purely compulsive, purely homicidal killing."

"I don't know. I haven't a clue yet. There seems to have been no physical connection between the two men. Thoday was a voluntary patient, and he was discharged, very much against our advice as it happens, more than a year before I engaged Vanek. I don't know, of course, what sort of motive you expect, but I do think it pretty unlikely that Peter Thoday would have been mixed up in anything of the remotest interest to you people." He turned his head as the door opened.

"Ah, there you are, Doctor, come in. This is General Kirk from the Foreign Office. General Kirk, Dr. Reade. Dr. Reade was the specialist in charge of Thoday while he was with us."

Dr. Reade was stout and smiling with blue eyes and white hair and she could have been described as a motherly body. As they shook hands, Kirk was reminded of scores of similar women he passed on Sundays shepherding children across the Park. She looked oddly out of place in Grace's masculine office.

She sat down opposite him and smiled benevolently as he repeated what he had said to Grace. When she replied her words were very thought out and considered.

"No, General, I don't think so. I don't think there could be any connection as you see it, and there need not have been anything that you or I would call a rational motive for what happened. You see, although I hardly knew Vanek, I seem to remember him as an almost exact opposite to Thoday.

"Yes, I knew poor Peter Thoday and that could just have been his motive."

She picked up the glass that Grace handed to her and smiled at him.

"I know that you'll disagree with my diagnosis, Doctor," she said, "but I'd like to tell General Kirk." She lifted the glass, drank from it, and for a moment looked at it as if it was a most rare and interesting object.

"Thoday was sent here from a private hospital as a depressive. He was an only son, living with his mother, and he had what almost amounted to religious mania. Of the Anglo-Catholic variety." She smiled again slightly.

"There was a long history of mental disease in the family, and some traces of hereditary syphilis, though I don't thing that that would have had much bearing on his case. He was admitted here after he had broken into a church and started playing the organ at two in the morning. Although he weighed under nine stone and stood five foot four, it took three policemen ten minutes to get him into the van.

"Well, I tried all the normal treatment for depressives on him. I even used insulin, but I didn't even scratch the surface of his trouble. I got no contact at all. It was as if there was no person here. Just an empty shell in which the yolk had died."

Kirk listened with deep attention. Very far back in his mind, a vague theory was beginning to form.

"He was only with us three months. As he was a voluntary patient, we couldn't keep him, and though I begged the mother to make him stay, she refused categorically. Her only theme was that once she got her boy home, the boy was thirty-two, all would be well.

"I'm afraid I bungled that case. I've still not the slightest definite idea of what he was suffering from and poor Peter Thoday is very much on my conscience. He wasn't a depressive, that's certain, but he may, just may have been a bad schitzo."

"Schitzo? Schizophrenic. I wonder if you would go into that with a bit of simple explanation, Doctor. I'm afraid I'm sadly ignorant of these matters." As he spoke an odd sense of embarrassment came over Kirk. The years seemed to slip away and he was once more back in the school-room, with a white-haired governess explaining the workings of Magna Carta.

"I'll try, General. It simply means a split mind, of course, but for what I want to get over, I'll put it another way. Tell me, have you ever been in a country which has just suffered military defeat?" She looked approvingly at Kirk's nod and went on.

"Good, then you may understand what I mean. One of my dearest friends is Austrian. She has often told me what it was like in Vienna in the days immediately following the First World War.

"She told me that on the surface people used to play a kind of game. They tried to pretend that everything was as before. Every broken institution existing as it always had done. It was only phantasy of course. On the lower, practical level there was hunger, chaos, often terrible violence. And between the two, there was something else. A kind of vacuum, a great emptiness, ready and waiting for another order to move in. Dr. Grace disagrees with me, I know. He says it is quite unscientific and savours of the occult. He is probably right, but I do honestly believe that in certain disorders a mind may become like that country and in it a vacuum waiting for an exterior force to fill it. Perhaps Thoday may have found that force, General Kirk."

"Thank you. And if you're right that could have given him the motive. Any idea what it might have been, Doctor?"

"Take your pick. It depends on the sort of things that Thoday was obsessed by. I only saw Vanek in passing, but I can think of five possibilities. He was a big man, he was rather handsome, he dressed flashily, he was a foreigner, he wore gold teeth. I don't know which, because I didn't have long enough with Thoday, and in any case it would probably have come after he left here.

"You see, four months after he went home, Thoday's mother died and he lived alone. She may have been an unpleasant woman, but she seemed to have had some kind of restraining influence. When he was alone, he might have been able to find the time and opportunity to fill that vacuum."

"Yes, he certainly might." Kirk lifted his glass and drank the last of the whisky. Then he stood up.

"Thank you both very much. What you've told me is most interesting, though I'm afraid I may have understood very little of it. Still, it does seem to confirm a vague theory of my own."

"Really, General, may we hear it?" Grace's big voice was as eager as a boy's.

"Of course you may, for what it's worth. You, Dr. Grace, put forward the idea that the psychological killer only attacks a certain type or group for which he feels fear or hatred. Dr. Reade tells us that in certain mental diseases there may be a vacuum which waits for something to fill it.

"I think you're probably both right. But in this case I don't believe it was anything either occult or psychological that possessed him. I think it was a real, flesh and blood, and very sane person.

"I'm staying in Tynecastle tonight, and in the morning I'm going to Thoday's house. Oh yes, I know the police have been through it already, but unless I'm wrong, I think I may find something. I think I'll find that after his mother died, Thoday made a friend. A new, but very dear friend who liked to help him. If that is the case, then I'll be a long way home.

"Once again, thank you both very much."

For the second time, he held Reade's warm hand and then followed Grace out of the door, and along the bright corridor which was vaguely reminiscent of the alley-way of a ship.

It was already dusk as he walked down the drive to the road. By the gates a stunted fruit tree leaned towards the dying sun in the west. The blight had eaten deep into it and it was drooping and ready for the axe. As he looked through its withered branches he felt a few drops of rain on his cheek. Cursing himself for dismissing his car in order to get some exercise, he set off quickly down the hill, past the gardens, the bright shops and the new villas into the gloom of the city centre.

As he walked, a great heaviness was all around him. He felt strangely alone and impotent. If Grace and that woman Reade were right, and he was almost sure they were, then he was up against something he couldn't deal with. A truly novel instrument of death. A means which would bring no throw-back, or retribution to its creator.

"Take a mind," he thought. "Take Thoday's mind, bleak and empty and purposeless, since his mother died. Go to him and make friends, and talk to him. Make friends and fill that empty space and possess him, and when you had done that, sit back and wait and smile. Wait, secure in the knowledge that after the action you had brought about, would come remorse."

He tried to picture the scene in the railway compartment. The unsuspecting bearer of news in his first class, corner seat, rolling up to London, for the promised reward. He saw the little man pulling open the door and seeing the monster in front of him. He saw him firing at the thing he hated and dreaded, and after that, the rest was not hard to imagine. The monster crumpling up in the seat and becoming just a dead human being. The cold, smoking gun in his hand and at every click of the wheels, his own mind clicking back to reality. And if you were Thoday. . . . If you were deeply alone and unhappy and friendless, there would be only one way out. No other hiding place. Only the door, held back by the wind, the quick leap towards the flying gravel, and to make doubly sure, a second tug at the trigger before it came.

He was in the centre of the city now. All around him, grim, smoke-blackened, pretentious, pile upon pile, the civic buildings frowned. In front of the portico of the Great Northern Hotel, Victoria sat on her stone chair, as on a commode. Kirk looked up at the sour, Hanoverian face and scowled.

"You flatulent old bitch," said the head of Her Majesty's Foreign Office Intelligence.

He was not late in going to bed. He dined poorly on underdone mutton and sodden greens and drank a glass of brandy. Then he played two games of snooker with the marker. It was barely ten forty-five when he went upstairs.

He closed the windows of his bedroom tightly, for he hated fresh air, and noted with satisfaction that a friendly chambermaid had given him an extra blanket. When he had got into bed, he smoked a final cigar and composed himself for sleep.

He had a selective mind, the capacity for opening or closing any thought chamber at will. Now he shut out all consideration of the case in hand, and let things go blank.

Sleep came quickly, but not deeply. He had no dreams, but there were pictures around him. Pictures of things and faces. His desk at Whitehall. Michael Howard. The rowing sculls over Grace's mantelpiece. Glyde. Always Glyde. From every corner of the dismal hotel bedroom, the boyish, smiling, inhuman face of the traitor seemed to stare at him.

And then the pictures faded. The walls themselves seemed to open, and he passed through them along a passage to another room. A big, dark room this time, and he was a child again, lying in bed, and watching the flickering shadows of a dying fire. And he was not alone in the room. Crouched by the fire, rocking backwards and forwards in front of it there was a woman.

She was an old woman, with a lot of grey hair, and her eyes were strange and bloodshot. She was looking at him, very intently, and she held something in her hands. He struggled against the image of his dream and waited for it to die. It didn't. If anything it seemed to grow stronger, and suddenly he was sitting upright in bed, knowing he was wide awake, while the big room shrank back to the hotel bedroom, the fire became the glow from a neon sign in the street and the chair stopped rocking.

Only the woman remained. She sat quite rigid in the chair, grey and haggard, mania in her eyes as she looked at him, and a shotgun in her hands.

"Hullo, James," she said. Her voice was dry and brittle, like something about to break. "So I've found you at long last, and now I'm going to kill you." The gun came up half an inch as she said it.

And all at once, Kirk knew that this was the second act, the repetition, the encore to the scene in the compartment.

He braced the bed-clothes around him, thanked God and the maid for his extra blanket and dived forward as Number Two fired.

CHAPTER FIVE

"Thank you very much indeed. Yes, that's all quite clear, and you'll let me have it in writing tomorrow. Thanks so much, goodbye."

Michael Howard replaced the phone and looked across the desk at Kirk.

"That was the report from the hospital about Mrs. Hill. It merely confirms what we already know, sir."

Kirk glowered at him. His normally reddish face was grey and sagging, and there was a long strip of plaster under his left eye.

"Does it, Michael? Does it really confirm what we know? How nice of it. And what the blazes do you consider it is that we already know?"

Michael grinned at his boss. He could quite sympathise with his ill-humour at the present moment.

"Well, we know about Mrs. Hill, sir," he said. "There has got to be a link between her and Thoday."

"Oh, yes, Mrs. Hill. Poor, dear Mrs. Hill. We know about her, do we? All I know is this. She was a small farmer's wife, who for fifteen years had been given a devil's own time by her husband. At the end of those fifteen years he clears off, leaving her destitute, and she takes a job as still-room maid at the Great Northern.

"The night I stay there, she takes a look at me. As soon as she finishes work she goes to her room, where she still keeps a few of her husband's things, and from them selects a sixteen bore shotgun. She then takes the pass key from the porter's office, and with the gun hidden in a sheet, gets into my room. As soon as I wake up she tries to get me with one barrel, which the blankets stop. Then she puts the other in her mouth and blows her head off.

"Well, that's all very helpful of her, Mike, but where exactly does it get us? We've heard what the police think. From her words to me before she fired, and from the fact that I seem to bear some slight resemblance to the deserting Mr. Hill"—he scowled at a photograph on the desk. "It would appear that she took me for him and was bent on retribution. So what!"

He got up and paced heavily backwards and forwards across the room.

"You know, up till today, I've been clinging to one definite theory. I felt there had to be something concrete behind all this. Some person, a new-found friend possibly, who had been using his influence on Thoday and Mrs. Hill, and playing on their mental situation to make them act as they did.

"Now we know that won't fit. These police reports knock it for six. Thoday and Hill were both retiring. They had few friends, certainly no new ones. There is nothing at all to suggest the kind of influence I had in mind. Mrs. Hill was not even psychotic. No hint of anything like that. Depressed, embittered, even revengeful perhaps, but there's no history of any mental disease. And yet she behaves almost exactly like Thoday." He pulled back his chair, and sat down again; there was a great weariness in his eyes.

"You know, Mike, we're getting nowhere. People just don't do these things."

Michael picked up the photograph and looked at it for a moment before replying.

"No, sir, they don't, do they? I think that may well be the whole point. You do look a little bit like him, you know. Two people so far. Two quiet people who suddenly go right off the handle, Thoday and Mrs. Hill. What made them do it? Thoday may well have been unbalanced, but if every nut behaved like he did, the world would be sadly depopulated. You are supposed to have been attacked because you resemble this woman's husband. That's one level, sir, the basement level. I think we should climb up and take a look at the ground floor."

"Go on, boy, if you think you're on to anything." Kirk raised his eyebrows and looked like a cross between John Bull and an ill-tempered chimpanzee.

"I think we should go back, sir, and start right at the beginning. I think that Vanek was killed, not only because he met a lunatic, but because he claimed to know something about Glyde. I think you were attacked by Mrs. Hill simply because you were interested in Glyde. I feel it's all as simple as that. Just Glyde, always

Glyde. His own sister told me she felt he might be still alive. She
had no facts, of course, just a feeling, and we can't go on it, but I
too feel quite certain about one thing. I think that alive or dead,
Glyde is the important factor. It may be he himself or just something about him, but it's very important. Important enough to
make someone very frightened and willing to stop at nothing to
keep it hidden." He took a cigarette from his case and lit it carefully before going on.

"By the way, sir. Have you heard, Kaltenheim comes out
tomorrow?"

"Yes, I have heard. I do keep in touch with current affairs,
Mike, however much it may seem to the contrary. And what
about Kaltenheim?"

"He's probably the last German contact we've got who actually knew Glyde. All the others are dead or disappeared. Couldn't
we talk to him?"

"Oh yes, certainly we can talk to him. We have done. I have,
that is. I talked to him for over a week, at the end of the war, and I
didn't get one single piece of information out of him.

"No, I'm afraid it would be useless, quite useless. That man
is probably the worst enemy either I or this country has got and
I'm very proud to say that it was largely on my testimony that he
got his fifteen years in Spandau prison. No, Mike, I doubt if we're
likely to learn a great deal from Herr Ernst von Kaltenheim."

"I realise that, sir. I phrased it wrongly. He wouldn't talk to us
of course, but I wonder if he could be persuaded to talk to someone he considered an ally. I wonder, for instance, if he might just
talk to say—Glyde's sister."

As they came towards it he remembered the city. He remembered it as it had been. The long roads running east like arrows.
The tell-tale loom of the Wannsee lakes, the searchlights and the
flak coming up, as years ago he had looked down from a Lancas-
ter and watched Berlin burning.

Now the blue Lufthansa plane came smoothly in. It wheeled
as it crossed the radio tower with the flags of the lost provinces
around it, and began the long sweep across Charlottenburg to the
dark rectangle of Tempelhof.

Michael glanced at Penny on the seat beside him, and there was something like love in his eyes as he looked at her. That and another thing. Bewilderment.

He hadn't even begun to scratch the surface of what she was. Beneath the facade of cynicism or love-making, he felt another self which he couldn't begin to share. A lonely, waiting creature, shut away from the daytime and completely self-contained. Waiting. Waiting perhaps for the same thing as Kirk. News of the boy who had gone away.

For a moment he felt he caught a glimpse of her other self behind the eyes as she watched the growing city. Then she turned to him and like a carnival mask her expression altered.

"Nice, very nice to travel on expenses," she said. "Your job, Mike? Pretty good isn't it? I mean financially of course."

"Mind your business," he grinned at her. "Not nearly as good as the used car trade, I should think, but nothing really is, is it? Seriously though, you're quite sure you know what you have to do?"

"What I have to say to this fellow Kaltenheim, you mean. Oh yes, I think so. I should do, after the way you and your boss have grilled me. In any case, it's too late for me to improve now. Here we are."

The landing wheels slammed into the tarmac in a harsh, screaming rush and the plane shot forward, slowed and wheeled round to draw up smoothly before the main immigration hall. They walked out at the end of the line of passengers, and as they came down the ramp, Michael smelt Berlin. Petrol, sweat, cigar smoke, and not so strong now, but still there, the thin, acid tang of rubble.

"Lang."

As promised, they had been met. Hans Lang clicked his heels, shook Michael's hand in a hard, jewelled grip, and to her joy, kissed Penny's. He was about five foot six, wore steel-rimmed glasses and looked like a benevolent gnome in his dark, rather boy scout beret.

"Strange," thought Penny. "Strange how they all look so very ordinary. This man must be Michael's opposite number, and yet neither of them would be noticed in a crowd."

Whatever his appearance, however, Lang carried authority. He flicked his beringed fingers at customs officers, immigration officials and policemen and within seconds they were sitting in the back of a waiting Opel.

"And now, where can I have the pleasure of driving you, my dear colleagues?" There was a huge crease of good humour in his crab-apple face. "May we first offer you some refreshment, or is it straight to work?"

"To work, I'm afraid, we had lunch in Hanover."

"In Hanover, so. A pity. That is a city which I have always thought one of the most detestable in Germany. Very well, we had better go and look at the ceremony."

"The ceremony? Sorry, old boy, I'm afraid I'm not quite with you."

"The ceremony, my dear Mr. Howard, or perhaps celebration would be a better word, to mark the release of one of the great martyrs of the National Socialist Party. Reichs Minister Ernst von Kaltenheim. Former Gauleiter of Essen. Former Chief of outside propaganda, answerable only to the good Dr. Goebbels himself. Former Organiser of all labour camps throughout the Ukraine. Now at last to be freed from his unjust imprisonment by the Nuremberg tribunal and restored to the bosom of his family and Fatherland. Oh yes, Mr. Howard, there is to be a celebration."

He gave a gruff order to the chauffeur and sank back against the cushions as the car moved off. Penny noticed that he smelt slightly of Chanel No. 5.

"And your good General Kirk, how is he. Excellent! My chief wished me to say he was sorry he couldn't meet you himself, but for obvious reasons it appeared to be undesirable. Actually, I myself know very little about this affair. All I have to do is to push you a little on your way and be of any assistance that I can. I will be able to get you into the Hotel Frankreich, where they are holding the reception for him, but once there it will be up to you." He turned in the seat and looked at Penny. For the first time, she realised that his eyes behind the thick lenses were very hard and shrewd.

"Tell me, gnaes Fräulein," he said. "Have you any real knowledge of the man you are going to meet?"

She shook her head. "Only the outline that General Kirk and Mr. Howard gave me, I'm afraid."

"And that, of course, would be very thorough. One thing I would like to impress on you, however. When you meet Kaltenheim, he may at first appear to be a rather stupid man; a bluff, hearty soldier, perhaps. Don't believe it, look very carefully at him, and you will see that he is a very bright boy. During the war, his intimates used to call him the Chameleon. That is why he got so light a sentence. He always contrived to appear as the man under orders, never the prime mover. He was quite as ruthless as any of the others, but because of that, he lived and they died. I think you will have to know your facts very well to make him believe you were sympathetic to your brother's actions. Do you for instance know what was the code name he used while with the radio department, Miss—Miss Glyde?"

"No, no, I'm afraid I don't." The use of that name came as a shock to her.

"It might be useful, you know. His intimates used to refer to him as Mr. S. F. That is how Kaltenheim would remember him, I think."

"Mr. S. F. What is the derivation?" She asked the question rhetorically. She was almost sure she could guess.

"Oh, it is not important. It comes from Schadenfreude. A word that I'm afraid is not translatable into the English language."

"No, you're quite right, we have happily no equivalent." She replied to him in faultless German. "Yes, that would be just the kind of word my brother would use. Schadenfreude, the joy felt at another's despair."

She turned away from his suffering, apologetic gnome's eyes and looked out at the rolling vistas of New Berlin.

And it *was* new. Like reaped grass, the city was growing again, the rubble shrinking, the empty windows filling, and the tall concrete buildings rising in the gaps like trees. They crossed the Zoo intersection, and the Kaiser Wilhelm Memorial Church, still preserved as a monument to pain. The Winged Victory statue, glittering in the sun with its French gun barrels and comic angel. Then up the long, marching, landing road of the East-West Axis, till at last they rattled over the cobbles and tram lines into the Spandauerdamm.

The prison was exactly what a prison should look like. It

crouched, low and gaunt, with decorative towers and a studded gate, resembling a pretentious version of Wandsworth jail. At the moment it was on holiday.

The police guards in front of the gate looked very smart and imposing in their grey uniforms and tall helmets. The sun glinted on their batons and sidearms but in one or two eyes there was a hint of fear as they looked at the crowd before them.

But crowd was a poor word for the group in front of the prison. It was too orderly, too quiet, too rigid. It was like a battalion of soldiers waiting for the start of a parade.

There was a big grey car to the right of the gate and a woman stood beside it between two silk-hatted members of the Bundestag. Along the road, drawn up in lines as an escort, were the troopers of the Stahlhelm, and behind them, drilled, unchattering, full of wonder, the flags of the provinces tight in their hands, Schlesien and Preussen, Sachsen and Brandenburg, were the children.

Lang leaned forward and spoke to the driver. Their car wheeled across the road and drew up in front of a little café, gay with painted tables and a striped awning. He opened the door and led them through the crowded bar and up a staircase to a small, very clean room, with chairs by the window and a decanter of clear liquid on the table. He darted forward and pulled back one of the chairs for Penny, waving her into it like a very fragile and valuable piece of property.

"Please sit down, my friends. I hope you like this room, I booked it for you, because I felt we could observe our quarry better from here than standing among that." He waved his hand towards the crowd and then turned to the table and filled three glasses.

"Well, Prosit. To the success of your mission, whatever it may be." He drained his Schnapps in a quick, practised motion.

Penny sipped hers slowly. She liked the strong, bitter Korn, but she treated it with respect. From the window she could look down on the crowd as from a theatre box or a grandstand, and as she looked, she remembered a similar scene years ago, when she had worked for a provincial paper, and been sent to witness the release of a wife-beater from Strangeways Prison.

Similar, and yet so different. The cold, damp morning with the mist swirling around the cobbled yard. The woman with her three children huddled by the wall out of the wind. The man coming slowly out from the postern and walking shamefacedly forward. The woman looking at him for a moment, her face working, beginning to turn away, and then rushing brokenly into his arms. It had no connection whatever with the sunlit release of Kaltenheim.

"I wonder what we have come into the wilderness to see, as the Hebrew Bible says?" said Lang at her side. "A reed broken by the wind? I wonder. We shall see."

And now something was happening. The guards stepped to the side. The Stahlhelm troopers came stiffly to attention. The faces of the children turned as one to the gate and from somewhere in the crowd, a band broke into the opening bars of "Deutschland über alles" . . . Then the side door slid back and into the sunlight came Kaltenheim.

He was very tall and erect, and even in the distance he didn't seem to have aged at all. His hair might have been a trifle thinner, he might have added a few pounds in weight, but it was the same man who in his time had graced the front pages of every major newspaper in the world. The same arrogant face looked out from the doorway as it had done from the Nuremberg dock, and neither his features nor his expression had altered.

For a fleeting second he stared at the crowd. Then his body stiffened, his feet flicked together and his right arm came forward in the National Socialist salute. For perhaps one minute he stood to attention as the battle hymn blared around him, then he walked quickly forward to the waiting group. He bent his head, kissed the woman and shook hands with the Bundestag dignatories, then he looked along the straight lines of the veterans.

"Thank you," he said. "Thank you, my comrades." He beckoned to his wife, and together they climbed into the grey car. The children burst through the cordon, cheering and waving their flags, as Kaltenheim bowed stiffly and smiled at them. The car pulled out into the road, and the ceremony was over.

"No, not a reed shaken by the wind, I'm afraid." Michael

smiled at Lang. "Hardly touched by it, in fact. Well, shall we get down to business? The reception will start at five, we were told."

"At five sharp, but I think it desirable that the Fräulein is not too punctual." He glanced at his watch, and then like a conjuror producing the final act, dived in his pocket and brought out a heavily embossed parchment card.

"Allow me, gnaes Fräulein, your invitation. Very tasteful, is it not? Very difficult to get, too. The reception is to be purely for the members of the family, and old comrades and their wives. I had to pay a lot of money in bribes for this little slip of paper." He smiled at Michael. "Doubtless my chief will be sending you his account before long, Herr Howard."

"Right, this is the plan of campaign that I have worked out. You have rooms booked at the Bristol Hotel in the Grunewald, I think? Good. It is quite comfortable and near the Frankreich, where they are holding the reception. I suggest you go there now. You will want to eat, and the Fräulein will have to change. Very formal this affair. I have arranged for a taxi to pick you up at five thirty. By that time most of the guests will have arrived and you will probably be taken for someone's wife or sister.

"Now, here is the important thing, Fräulein. If you are to get anything out of Kaltenheim, I don't know what you want, but if you are to get him to talk, you will have to play your cards exactly right.

"You are the sister of John Glyde. I know that that is correct because I have been told; but will Kaltenheim know? Perhaps you have papers or photographs to prove it. Good, excellent. Now, Fräulein, what is not correct. What I hope is not correct, but which you must make him believe, is that you fully approve of your brother's actions. That you feel well disposed towards him, and out of respect for his memory, you wish to hear his story from the lips of his former superior. Right, is that all quite clear?" Once more, through the glasses, she made out the sharp, efficient mind behind the gnome-like expression.

"Very well, now I am afraid it is better that we should part company for a little while. My car will take you to the Bristol, and you will of course phone me if you require further assistance." He smiled. "I hope you will, in any case. I would very much like to hear how you get on."

He jumped to his feet, bowed to Penny as he opened the door, and watched them paternally as they went down the stairs to the waiting car.

The Hotel Frankreich stood at the end of the Koenigsallee, a long, winding street, that led through the pine forest they called the Green Wood, and which had been a sort of millionaires' row before the war. It had been badly damaged in the street fighting, but now its former inhabitants were coming home, and the mock palaces rising again. They were in every style of architectural perversity, from glass cubes to Gothic spires, and they were tightly packed in small gardens fenced with wire. Berlin had shrunk since the war, and ground rents were enormously high. The inhabitants of the Grünewald seemed to live in a kind of plutocratic caravan settlement.

The taxi deposited Penny a little way from the entrance of the hotel, among a collection of some of the most magnificent cars she had ever seen. For a moment the job in hand faded and she eyed them lovingly, and with avarice in her heart.

"Just half a dozen of you," she thought. "No, not as many, just two of you beauties, safely tucked away in the mews garage and we leave the Thorntons for ever, and go up into real money class." She drew her hand along the scarlet bonnet of a Mercedes and walked reluctantly to the entrance.

The doorman of the Frankreich was blue and gold and impressive as one of Frederick's tall grenadiers. He looked Penny up and down and stepped in her way.

"My apologies, Fräulein," he said. "I am afraid the Hotel is not open to the general public this evening."

"Oh, dear, I'm so very sorry. I didn't realise that I looked like the general public." She produced the embossed card with a flourish and smiled sweetly, as she watched him shrivel.

"Oh pardon. A thousand pardons, Madame. You see, I have strict orders to admit no one except members of the reception and most of the guests have already arrived. Schmidt, schnell." With a deft, almost feminine dexterity he performed three complex motions in one, bowing deeply from the waist, removing her coat, and flicking his fingers at a bowed, aged and incredibly tiny figure who scurried crabwise across the hall towards them.

"The boy will take you up, Madame, once more please accept my apologies." Again came the musical bow, and Penny followed the boy up the thickly piled stair carpet, smiling as she went.

"Invoice," she thought grimly. "Herr Ernst von Kaltenheim, in account with Frankreich Hotels Ltd. To foot licking of guests, 50 Deutsche Westmark."

The reception hall was long and low and seemed to be made entirely of glass and chrome steel. There were probably less than a hundred guests present, but the mirrors made them look like a multitude.

"Good evening, Fräulein. Allow me to introduce myself." The man by the door clicked his heels, bowed and made a number of guttural noises that sounded like insults. He was tall and beautiful and he had a completely vacant face that only his monocle seemed to hold together.

"Ah, Fräulein Wise." He pronounced it with a V. "And what may I get you to drink, gnädige Fräulein?" His hand shot out arresting a waiter in flight.

"Champagne, please, and it's Frau Wise." Penny took a deep, greedy gulp from her glass. The atmosphere of the room was overpowering.

"So, a pity." He leaned gallantly over. "But why haven't we met before, my dear Frau Wise? I thought I knew all the friends of the Reichsminster." He used the title blandly and without hint of embarrassment. "And I can assure you I would have remembered your face."

"Thank you. I am afraid I do not know Herr von Kaltenheim personally, though he was kind enough to send me an invitation. He knew my family in London when he was with your embassy."

"Really. So you are English, how interesting. Your German is remarkably good, though I did notice a slight trace of accent. English, eh. I am a great admirer of your nation, gnädige Frau. As you are here, you must be one of us, so you will appreciate the destroying influences to which you have been subjected since Oliver Cromwell. However, I still feel that in both blood and basic culture we can be called brother peoples."

"Basic culture!" She raised her eyebrows slightly at that one.

"But natürlich. The whole basis of your language, for instance; German, Anglo-Saxon, with a smattering of Norman French. The great Shakespeare was, of course, of German descent. You are perhaps acquainted with the work of our national poets, gnädige Frau, Goethe, Wagner, Schiller."

"Yes, Schiller." She turned away from this idiotic creature, hoping to catch a glimpse of Kaltenheim in the crowd.

"Yes, I have read some Schiller, a wonderful poet, we call him Shelley in English."

"Shelley, so, that is most interesting. I did not know they were the same person. Allow me, I must make a note of that." He pulled a leather diary and pencil from his pocket and laboriously made his note.

"Ah, Hans, there you are, please introduce me to your friend."

Frau von Kaltenheim was even smaller and more bent than she had seemed at the prison. For the party, she had changed into a vivid blue dress and used make-up lavishly. Neither could conceal the worn lilies of her face and body. Only her eyes seemed alive. They were bright and intelligent and they stared suspiciously at Penny.

"Good evening, Magda." The tall man pushed the diary back into his pocket. "Allow me to present Miss—sorry, Mrs. Wise from England. She tells me the Reichsminister is an old friend of her family."

"Really, that is interesting. I'm afraid I do not recall your face. Where did my husband meet your parents, my dear?"

"When—when he was first secretary at the London embassy in thirty-seven." Michael's briefing stood her in good stead.

"I see. That, of course, was before we were married, but I don't remember sending you an invitation." The words were said without hint of threat or suspicion. They were just a statement. Only the sharp eyes spoke.

"Your husband was kind enough to send me one personally from Spandau."

"Oh, I see. How like him. He has always had very strong memories for his old friends of the past. He is not in this room just now, he was very tired, so I made him rest for a little. Still, I'm sure he will want to see you. Come and meet him, my dear. You will excuse us, Hans?"

"But of course. I hope you will come back to me, Mrs. Wise. It is very pleasant to discuss cultural topics with members of other nations."

Penny smiled at him and followed her hostess through the room to a door at the end. She knocked three times and then pulling it back led Penny forward. There was great strength in her tiny hand.

"Ernst," she said. "Here is the daughter of some old friends in England who wishes to see you."

Von Kaltenheim sat at a desk with a cigar in his hand. He got up and bowed politely as Penny entered.

"Your family were friends of mine, you say. Yes, the face does seem familiar, my dear, but I just can't think of the name. No, no, don't tell me. Please let me think for a moment."

His expression was gentle and friendly and slightly stupid, but his mouth was the cruellest thing she had seen on a human being. It was just a slit, a gash. There was no other way to describe that lipless mouth, which spoke so politely to her and which might have been cut with a razor on the tight bladder of his face. Above it the eyes glowed with a film of good humour and kindness, but it was just a film, a trick of light. Behind them, she sensed the fearful thing that had made the mouth the shape it was.

"Perhaps I may have known your father while I was with our embassy in London." There were deep furrows in his brow as he looked at her.

"No, no, Herr Reichsminister." To her surprise, the title came quite easily. "No, you didn't know my father, and I'm afraid I am more or less a gatecrasher at your reception. You see, it was my brother you knew. You need to call him Mr. S.F."

And that went home; it hit Kaltenheim bang in the centre of the bullseye. He seemed to sway slightly, even the mouth went slack and for the merest hundredth part of a second she saw clearly the thing behind his eyes. Then his face came together and he turned to his wife.

"Magda, Magda, my dear, will you leave us alone for a

moment. Thank you." He waved Penny into a chair and stood in front of her.

"Now, you claim that you are Glyde's sister. Will you kindly prove it."

Without speaking, Penny opened her bag and handed him the three photographs Michael had told her to bring. For a long time he looked at them and then, with a stiff bow, passed them back. As she watched him she suddenly saw that the rigid youthful air he had carried that afternoon was just a pose. Under the military bearing, the stiff shoulders, yes, and the powdered made-up face, there was just a tired old man who had done fourteen years in prison.

"Yes, you are Glyde's sister. I believe you, and moreover I am sorry for you. Well, to business. What do you want of me?"

"Herr von Kaltenheim. Can't you see? Can't you understand what I want? I want to know. I was only a child when John went to Paris. All my life has been haunted by his actions. It is now a long time since he gave his last broadcast, but please tell me what happened to him. I must know what became of him since he disappeared." There was not a trace of acting in her words.

"Yes, I see that. I see that quite clearly. But, as you say, it is a long time." He flung himself down in an armchair opposite her and relit his cigar.

"My dear, what I am going to tell you will probably hurt. When I first knew your brother I was in charge of all propaganda broadcasts from Radio Hamburg. He was sent to me, at first, purely as an announcer. Later he became a script writer and producer. His programmes were by far the most effective we ever managed to put on. That was the trouble with him, they were too good.

"You see, these things work both ways. It is like poison gas or germ warfare. If one side uses it so will the other. With our enormous losses in Russia, we had no desire for the British to start the same kind of stuff your brother was putting over, therefore he was told to alter the tone of his broadcasts. He agreed at once, on one condition. He was to be allowed access to British prisoner of war camps for the purpose of propaganda. It was then that he got his nickname and also at about that time that he began to change."

"To change." Penny sat quite rigid in her chair staring at him.

"Yes, Fräulein, to change." He paused for a moment and carefully dropped the ash from his cigar. When he continued, his words were very quiet and distant.

"I am a real German, my dear. A Hitler German. I regret nothing I did because it was done for my leader and my country. With your brother it was different. The end did not matter to him, only the means, the interest. Yes, the means of destroying a personality, that was his cause. I watched him once, with a prisoner. It was a young boy, a merchant seaman, I seem to remember. Your brother just sat and talked to him. It didn't matter what he said, the words signified nothing. It was something else. It was as if there was an invisible wire stretched between the two of them along which something was passing from your brother to the prisoner. At the end of half an hour that boy was like putty in our hands. That was the change I meant. It was something I didn't understand, something inhuman, almost unphysical. No, I didn't understand it, but you know, I feared it. I, Ernst von Kaltenheim, feared it."

And fear was round Penny too now. It was all worse, so much worse. The broadcasts were nothing compared to this. This was horrible. But even through the horror there was hope. At every word of Kaltenheim she felt she was getting closer in her search. Her search, which though controlled by Kirk and Michael, was still personal. Right or wrong, knave or devil, it was her search. The search for John.

"And then," she said. "What happened to him then?"

"Then he started to decay. It was a physical, moral, intellectual decay. There was drinking, women, drugs, even boys. He was repeatedly getting into fights in the Reeperbahn clubs. In one of them a waitress hit him with an ice pick and his left hand was badly injured. We had a special guard with him all the time at the end.

"The last broadcast was on August 10th, '44. As soon as he had finished it, he collapsed. He was completely paralysed. I had him sent with this guard, who had become a sort of personal attendant, to a mental home near Munich. That was the last time I saw him. Ten days later I received personal orders from

Himmler himself. Your brother was to be presumed dead. All papers relating to him were to be destroyed. It was a treasonable offence to even mention his name. That, I am afraid, is all I know. I am a good German and I obey orders. You are the first person with whom I have discussed Glyde since I received Reichsführer Himmler's instructions." He pulled himself up from his chair to signify the end of the interview.

"And there is no one else who would know more? The staff at the mental home, for instance."

"No one, Frau Wise; he was transferred from there to a hospital which was bombed by your air force in the November; there were few survivors."

"But the guard, the personal attendant you spoke of. Is he alive, do you know his name?"

"The guard. Yes, he was a Sudeten Czech, I think. It's a long time and I can't be sure. No, I can't be sure, but I think his name was Vanek."

CHAPTER SIX

"Yes, Mr. Howard, I think we may be in luck." Lang bent over his big, steel-backed reference files and his gnome's face was alive with efficiency.

"They do themselves well," thought Penny. "Very well in the Spionage Abwehr Dienst of the West Deutsche Bundes Republik."

She looked round the room and compared it most favourably with the gloomy cage Kirk called his den. It was cream and gold, and bright with concealed neon lights and flower prints. It had sham alabaster ashtrays and a blonde secretary in a tight black costume. She didn't use Odorono, but looked as if she would possibly compensate for that in other ways.

Only Lang himself was out of place. He still wore his beret, and there was a greenish haze on his suit. He hadn't shaved for some time and he could have been sitting on a tree stump, waiting for the lost traveller in a Grimm's Fairy Tale.

"And only man is vile," said Penny suddenly, aloud in English.

"Pardon, gnaelige Frau." Lang looked up with a jerk.

"Oh, nothing. I'm so sorry, I was merely thinking aloud." She blushed deeply and turned her head from Michael's wink.

"So, well, as I said, we are fortunate." Lang pushed the files away from him.

"It seems that your Herr Vanek did visit Berlin. He stayed one night in a hotel on the Kantstrasse. We have here his registration card. We also have a copy of the form he had to fill in when he arrived at Charlottenburg station. He is probably quite frank about the purpose of his visit. He gives as his reason a wish to see his brother, Paul Vanek, at present resident at Number 32 Lutzow-allee, Leipzigerstrasse. That is unfortunately just inside the Russian Sector of the city."

"Thank you." Michael scribbled the address in his diary. "Well, Herr Lang, what is the best method of getting to Lutzow-allee? I suppose the Underground to the Potsdamer Platz?"

"Yes, that would be the best route to take normally, but in your case I would strongly advise against it. You see, Herr Howard, things are very quiet now. We haven't had any incidents with our friends in the East for several months. It is perfectly all right for ordinary citizens to go in and out of their sector. But would you, my friend, describe yourself as an ordinary citizen? No." He shook his head.

"No, Mr. Howard, these people are not fools. It is ten to one than you would not be questioned, but if you were, and they became even vaguely suspicious of your occupation, then I'm afraid our General Kirk would shortly be deprived of a most valuable assistant. Now, what I suggest is this. You wish to see this man Vanek. Right, we shall send for him. I have a friend in the Vopo, the People's Police, a Major Klein. I shall telephone him and ask him, with a promise of something, to bring Vanek to the neutral ground by the Brandenburger Tor. There you can have your interview in complete safety."

With a smile Michael got up and held out his hand.

"No, I am afraid that would be putting you to too much trouble, Herr Lang. Besides, if Vanek is to tell me anything I want to know, I will have to take him by surprise. No prepared interviews, I think. There is one thing you can do for me, however, and that is to entertain Mrs. Wise while I am gone."

"Oh no, you don't. Much as I would like to be entertained by Herr Lang, I'm coming too. Didn't you hear your boss make me a kind of deputy Sheriff. Oh no, Comrade Howard. If you're going anywhere on this trip, you take me too."

Penny stood up, pulled her coat around her shoulders and moved to the door. Michael started to protest, then looked at the set of the mouth and gave it up. He grinned sadly at Lang and followed her.

It was only the advertisements that told them they were there. In the five earlier stations they might have been in any underground railway system anywhere. There were the same pictures of girls in bras, the same cold-cures, the same cigarettes. Somebody's perm, somebody's motor cars, somebody's fruit drops. And suddenly the advertisements stopped altogether and became political slogans and posters of hard-faced men in uniform. "United Front against Fascism and War." "Rebuild our City without Marshall Aid." "Glory to Comrade Peick." "We have enough trees in East Berlin to hang every Western War-Monger." Penny frowned slightly at that one.

Lutzo Walle was battered and unlighted and full of pot holes. There had been little rebuilding in the East except for the H.O. communal stores, the government offices and the stage facade of Stalinallee. The street along which they walked was still a line of ruins, and through its gaps, they could see the real wasteland of the town, with its heaps of fallen masonry like tall sand dunes, reaching out to the new buildings of the West.

As they walked, they both felt the loneliness of Berlin. The glittering centre round the Zoo and the Kurfuerstendamm was just a game, just a trick, a dot in the wilderness. All around it lay the broken earth, the cracked concrete roads, and the allotments running east. Running all the way east across the untilled plains to the Pacific.

Number 32 was still partly intact. Half of it had vanished, and high up on a party-wall, a lavatory pan hung incongruously against the sky. There was still a hall though, with stairs going up and a board with Vanek P. indicated on the first floor.

Michael knocked on the door and stood back as it creaked

open, and a woman peered out at him through the gloom. From inside the flat they could hear a child crying.

"Well, what do you want?" The woman's voice was not so much hostile as guarded and full of fear. She was thin and bent, and her feet were wrapped in rags.

"We are friends, madame." Michael's voice was warm and full of forced charm. "Friends of Herr Vanek's brother. He gave us this address."

"His brother. His brother from England. I know him. And you are from England too?" She turned from Michael and looked hard at Penny. Staring at her face, her coat, her costume and her shoes, above all her shoes. It was with a shock that Penny realised that this bent creature was a young woman of about her own age. She saw the deep fear in her eyes, the hesitation of giving away any information which might compromise her, and without speaking, flicked open her bag and pulled out a nearly full packet of cigarettes.

It worked beautifully. A hand, thin as a child's, groped forward to take them and a look of understanding came into the face. "Thank you," she said, "thank you, Fräulein Engländerin. You will find him at the Fat Sow Café in Französische Strasse. You will always find him there. He almost lives there." Her hand shot out, reached for the packet and, tucking it into the folds of her torn dress, she turned back to the door. Just before she reached it, she stopped and looked at Penny again.

"You will get nothing from him, you know, Fräulein Engländerin," she said. "It is past ten. He will be drunk. He is always drunk by ten. He will be no good to an English lady after ten, that I promise you, Fräulein. I, his wife, promise you, Fräulein, he will be no good." She smiled an aged, bitter smile at her, gathered something in her mouth and vanished through the door. It had already closed when the thin spittle fell around Penny's feet.

She was quite right. Vanek was drunk, dead drunk. The piano top in front of him was covered with slops and half empty glasses and his eyes seemed to look across the smoke of the room as from a long way off and under water. He was still serviceable, though, his hands moved like lightning over the keys and the harsh, metallic music thundered around the small, prefabricated building.

Michael led Penny across the bare, unplaned boards of the dance floor and took the table by the piano. He ordered a bottle of white wine and looked around him. As he had thought, the "Fat Sow" was not particular in its clientele.

It was as near a thieves' kitchen as was possible to imagine. The Teddy boys and girls on the floor were dressed as their English colleagues, but their faces would have made Brixton look like a garden suburb. And they were the least. All around the walls sat the others. The tired, elderly whores who had not even bothered to make up. The lean men in every type of ragged civilian dyed uniform. All watching them. All silent, unsmiling, waiting, waiting with their lean, hard, rather scholarly faces fixed and hostile.

As the music died, he turned and looked at the pianist. He was shocked at what he saw, for it was like looking at a ghost. It was too near. Just four days had passed since he had seen that face, three-eyed against the first class railway cushions, and now he was with it again. The same broad forehead, the heavy lower lip, everything as before. But it had looked better dead. Much better. There had been a slight nobility about that face in death. Now it was utterly horrible. The red, and yet still liquid eyes, the convulsive twitch, the transparent beads on the forehead. All the trappings of decay.

"Yes," he thought. "Drink, drugs, women, the lot. Your wife's quite right, old boy. No good to any English lady now."

He bowed to Vanek's brother and smiled. "I enjoyed your playing very much," he said. "I wonder if you'd join us for a drink?"

"So, you would like to buy me a drink." His words were slurred and indistinct, but behind the broken flesh of the body the mind seemed clear and active. It was only the mind that held him together.

"What would you like to buy me? New wine, sugared water, anything else? No, there is nothing here that I would care to drink with a foreigner, so thank you for your civility and No."

"No, not wine, I have something else." Michael took a flat, silver flask from his pocket and put it on the table. "Something that I think you might like, Herr Vanek."

"So, you know my name. I wonder who could have given it to you. Perhaps you have been speaking to the Director of the

Philharmonische Orchestra, is that it? 'You must pay a visit to the Fat Sow Café when you are in Berlin. Wonderful place, brilliant clientele.' " His hand waved jerkily around the room and the terrible faces.

' "And the music, my dear fellow, you can have no idea how good the music is. Chap called Vanek, what a pianist, a real artist. You will be in for a musical treat.' "

He got up from his stool and came down the two steps to the table. Every ounce of concentration he had was needed to control his lurching feet.

"Now let us see what you have in this very nice toy." He poured himself a generous glass and threw it back in a single quick movement. Almost at once his face grew firmer and his colour began to change.

"Scotch, very good. You are British. I thought so. I have never had such a drink as this since we chased your armies out of France in forty-one. God! how you ran." He refilled his glass again, lifted it mockingly towards Penny and then looked very hard at Michael.

"Well, you know my name, what do you want of me—sir. In Berlin it is always better to call foreigners Sir."

"I want you to tell me something, Vanek. I want to know the question your brother asked you ten days ago, and I want to know your reply."

"Ah, so you are acquainted with my brother, are you. How nice for him. Couldn't he tell you himself what his very simple question was? He paid well for it, very well for him. Nearly three hundred German marks, West. How well can you pay, Mr.—Mr. Howard. Thank you. A good English name, Howard, isn't it."

"Nothing, Vanek, pay nothing. Nothing at all, but I will tell you something in return. Because of what you told him, your brother died, he died four days ago with a bullet in his head."

Michael had expected some reaction to his statement, not much perhaps, certainly not grief, but at least some slight sense of shock. What came was terrifying, for Vanek laughed. He roared with laughter, he struggled up from his seat and shook with it, knocking the glass over as he did so. The tears ran down his cheeks on to his grey tie-less collar as he laughed.

"So it worked," he shouted, "after all these years it did work. He was right. I told him it was impossible. It couldn't have been what he thought, and he was right, right all the time. Bang in the centre of the target." The words came gasping out through the ripples of his mirth.

He made a great effort, straightened and shouted across the room to one of the grey men by the wall.

"Toni, take over the piano, will you? Just for ten minutes. I have business in the office, business with two rich friends from England." Still choking with laughter, he beckoned them to follow him and led them through a curtain to a dark oil-lit room behind the stage.

"Well, sit down, my dear friends. I'm afraid the furnishings are not of the best, but we have homely comforts." His thin hand swept the cracked lino, the rickety chairs, the peeling wallpaper and came to rest on a tall bottle on the table. He lifted it to his lips, drank deeply from it and then slumped down opposite them.

"Yes, because you have made me laugh, I will answer those two questions when you have done one thing more for me. Tell me this, Herr Howard. Who killed my brother? No, no, that is wrong. Not who. What? What killed him? Was it by any chance a member of the insane?"

With complete bewilderment Michael nodded. Nothing made sense any more, nothing fitted, nothing really mattered. He was in a dream world where the shapes were only shadows and this laughing creature was the centre of the dream.

"Yes, as I thought. As I told him it might be. Poor Stephen, poor soft, foolish Stephen. I will tell you about him, shall I? Yes, but first, have you perhaps a cigarette? Thank you—"

He lit the cigarette and inhaled deeply, his body bent in concentration. For a minute he seemed to have no object in life other than drawing the last atom of pleasure from that one cigarette.

"Imagine a country town, Mr. Howard, a small, sleepy country town, almost a village really. It has the musical name of Karlovy Varly, and it is on holiday. Today the streets are full, and the people are holding flags. Most of them. Some are going away. A few of them have handcarts and wheel-barrows piled with possessions and they are walking south. Outside the town there is a small hill.

Two boys are standing on it. They are arguing about something. Arguing bitterly. For a long time the argument goes on and then it is interrupted by a noise. A far-off drone, a rumble. They turn towards the noise and look towards it, then they shake hands and walk away. One of them turns south towards the crowd of refugees and the other runs down the hill to welcome the German tanks as they drive into Czechoslovakia."

"You and your brother."

"Yes, Stephen and I. That was in thirty-eight. He went to Prague and then by way of France to England. He died because he tried to meddle with something he didn't understand and I, I live, don't I?" He smiled suddenly and in his smile was all the bitterness of what he had to live with. The scarecrow in the Lutzowalle, the bottle, the Fat Sow and its customers.

"Yes, you live, and what you have told me is very interesting, but you still haven't answered my question, Herr Vanek."

"No, I haven't, have I, but give me time. 'Patience and time, time and patience,' as Tolstoy said. It was two years after the war when I saw Stephen again. Since the day we parted, I never thought about him. I considered him to be a traitor both to himself and his country. I still think that, Herr Howard. He felt otherwise, it seems. After the war he looked for me and he found me. He came here and we sat in this very room talking about old times. Old times and our war experiences. 'Those old, unhappy far-off times and battles long ago.' I didn't see him again till he came back the week before last."

"Yes, but my question. What did he ask you?"

"This. He asked me if I recognised this." He reached in his pocket and threw something on the table. "I said I did and that is all I said. That is the answer to both your questions, I think."

The photograph was dirty and crumpled. It had been rubbed among coins and keys and dust, but the picture was still clear. It showed a hand, a broad, rather capable hand with long fingers and it was open on a white surface. The palm was uppermost and it was the palm that was interesting. It had faint lines that showed nothing of character, but it had something more. Right in the centre, dark and kidney shaped, indistinct in the crumpled gloss, but definite as a stigmata, an inch across, there was a hole.

Michael picked it up and glanced sham casually at it. In the back of his mind a vague theory was beginning to fit. Everything was beginning to fit like pieces of a child's magnetic puzzle clicking metallically together.

"Yes," he said. "We know about that. He got it in forty-four, didn't he. You see we have friends, Vanek. Important friends. Von Kaltenheim told us."

"So you know Herr Ernst von Kaltenheim, whom may Hell be hot for. You know a lot, don't you. But you're quite right. A barmaid put an ice pick through his hand. Tell me, Mr. Howard. Just who are you?"

"He is nobody, nobody at all. Just a friend of the family." Penny leaned forward and touched the man's ragged sleeve. "It's I you want to think about now. Who am I, that is the question now, Vanek."

For the first time he seemed to take her in. Before, she had been just an appendage of Michael, something to bow to, to smirk at, to envy the possession of, nothing more. Now she was real. He stared at her for a moment and then his hand crept forward and tilted her head towards the light. His fingers were like a damp chammy leather, just pulled out of the sink.

"Yes, I see it. I do know. You have the same face. Who are you? Perhaps the sister. He told me he had a sister."

"You're quite right, Mr. S.F. did have a sister, and now you are going to talk to her. You are going to talk about everything you know about him, and you are going to talk quickly. Right, Vanek, what happened to my brother, what happened to John Glyde?"

And then it came. Once more he lifted the bottle and drank deeply. When he put it down again and looked at her, his face seemed to slacken and they saw he was really drunk. He started to speak and his words were blurred and indistinct and seemed to come from far away in the past.

"He wanted to die," he said. "Months before your air force bombed the hospital he wanted to die. But they wouldn't let him. He couldn't walk by then. He couldn't see. He just wanted to finish with it and they stopped him, and made him change. Yes, they made him change, change completely. God, the things they did to him to bring about the change. I used to push him out in a chair, and it was like being with a corpse in the burning.

"They said it was for the cause, you see. They said that he would be the weapon, the means of assassination. I didn't believe them then. I saw what was happening to him, and I still didn't believe them. I didn't believe Himmler himself, or even Doctor Rhine. Now it seems they were right." He looked up at Penny and he was like a child begging for forgiveness. '

"You see, we had to try everything. We had to get those men. It was forty five and we had to try everything. I worked with them all the time, right through till we cured the paralysis and they took him to the U Booo—"

They never saw the knife till it was home. There was no smooth curve through the air, no flash of metal in the lamplight. Nothing at all. Just the dark handle like an overgrown boil in the neck, the body whistling as it fell and the repeat in death. "Till they put him in the U—"

The next instant, Michael was on his knees beside him tilting his face to the light. It only needed the barest glance to see that Vanek was dead. He looked at the curtain hoping to detect a movement that would show him which way the knife had come, but apart from a slight tremor from the rising air it was quite still. No, not that way. He looked wildly around the room searching for a possible hiding place and then stiffened as Penny whispered in his ear.

"Mike, don't look round quickly, but to the left there is a window. Look at the window, Mike."

Very slowly he raised his head and turned to the left. She was right. There was a window. It was small and narrow and there was a bar across it. It was quite innocent except for one thing; it had a hand. High up and clutching the frame as if nailed to it, there was a hand.

He turned from the body and moved towards it. There were four paces to go. Four paces with his heart pounding and the boards hard under his knees. Just three paces and at any moment the hand might leave the window and he would never know how Vanek had died. Two paces and that or worse. There could be another knife in that expert hand and then—one pace, just one pace, just thirty-six inches and he was there. He braced himself on the floor, sprang at the hand, bent it hard back on the wrist and pulled.

It was too easy. Before he had even taken the weight he knew it was too easy. The body was too still, too light and unresisting. With one hand he pulled it forward till the face was resting against the sill in front of him and it was just another act, another movement of the game he didn't understand. Like Thoday, this killer had played it to the end. The act, the remorse, the second death. He looked down from the thin, almost childish face to where the second knife gleamed dully in the chest. Then he slowly released his hand and watched the body sprawl forward into the dust of the alley.

A second later there was a scream from Penny behind him, running steps on the boards and angry voices around him. He tried to turn, then felt the hands on his shoulder and was pulled backwards through the curtain. The next moment he was fighting for his life.

The boy came quietly, even daintily into the room and he was very tall and beautiful in his blue 'VOPO' uniform. He looked about eighteen, but he had the level eyes of a veteran. He smiled at the struggling group by the curtain and he didn't act at once.

"There is no need to hurry," he thought, "let them damage themselves a little." He hated hurry, so very slowly, as if the exertion was too much for him, he unslung his machine pistol and pointed it at the floor. He had to fire two short bursts before the fight broke up.

"Good, thank you very much. That is better. You will now all stand by the wall with your hands on your heads. All of you, women as well. Sergeant."

"Sir?" The sergeant had a tired elderly face and he could have been the boy's father. He quailed before him as before a general.

"If any person in this room moves without my permission, you are to shoot, Sergeant. That is an order. Now, who is in charge here?"

"Here, Herr Hauptman, at your service, Herr Hauptman." The manager wore a soiled white jacket and he bowed deeply.

"So, and what is the meaning of this disturbance? We heard it right across the street. You are doubtless aware of the penalties." He bit the corner of his lip as he said that.

"Yes, of course, Herr Hauptman. I know and I am sorry, but I think there has been a murder. It was that one there; the foreigner. He came in and spoke to Vanek, the pianist. They went into the back room together. They were there perhaps ten minutes when we heard a noise and went through. Vanek was lying on the floor and I think he is dead. We pulled this man back into the hall and were trying to restrain him when you were good enough to come in, Herr Hauptman."

"I see." He threw the barest glance at Michael and then walked across the room and through the curtain. He wasn't long, two minutes at the most. When he came back he was still smiling and there was a cigarette hanging from his lower lip. He came and stood close to Michael and he looked very friendly.

"Your papers, please. Thank you so much. I see, an Englishman. How nice to meet you—sir." He stuffed the passport into his tunic and lifted his hand. There was a solitaire ring on the index finger. It gleamed dully in the thick atmosphere and then came down like a whip across Michael's face.

"Now—will you please—tell me why—you killed the musician—sir." At each pause, the hand rose and fell through the air.

"I never touched him." Michael watched the sergeant's gun and he forced himself to keep his head rigid under the blows. "We were merely talking when somebody threw a knife from the window. If you look outside that window you will find the killer's body."

"That is a lie, Herr Hauptman. I swear it. I looked outside the window and there is nothing, nothing at all." The manager fussed like a dog at his side.

"Really, then I think we had better have a chat with my superiors, Herr Englander." The officer lowered his hand and reached in his pocket. The handcuffs were of blue gun-metal and there was a curious bulge at the base of each ring.

"Your hands, please. Thank you. While we are on the way to Headquarters, I would strongly advise you not to struggle. Our handcuffs are of a contracting pattern and are spring loaded. Any sudden movement causes them to tighten, sometimes with interesting results. I once saw a drunkard almost sever his wrist in that manner." He swung round to the men at the door.

"You two. Kirchmeyer and Wesel. You will remain here till the van arrives. You will see that nobody leaves. The man was alone when he came here, Herr Manager?"

"No, he wasn't alone. I was with him." Penny ignored both Michael's eyes and the sergeant's gun and stepped out from the wall. "I was with him all the time he was talking to Vanek. He had nothing to do with the knifing."

"So. An English lady, as well. How charming." He bowed deeply. "I have never spoken to an English lady, but I remember one once. It was a long time ago and she was sitting on the terrace of your officers' club in the Heerestrasse. She was eating kidneys and when she saw me watching her through the railings she took one off her plate and threw it at me. It rolled in the dust, but I picked it up and ate it. She laughed when she saw me eat it. I have never forgotten that laugh, Fräulein Engländerin."

"Sergeant. You and I will take these to the Bureau." He turned on his heel and walked to the door.

Michael sat quite rigidly in the front of the car beside the driver. He knew the strength of the things on his wrists and at each slight jolt he could feel the springs tensing. He was quite numb with the blows in his face and the knowledge of his own stupidity. Above the hum of the motor, Lang's words kept repeating and repeating themselves to him. "And would you describe yourself as an ordinary person, Herr Howard?"

He looked up at the twin windscreen mirror in front of him and watched Penny. For a moment he thought it was a trick of light and then knew it was true, for she was smiling.

She was leaning back against the cushions and smiling at the boy. The top button of her costume had come undone and there was a lot of breast showing. The boy's eyes had lost their hardness and they kept flicking towards it.

"Captain," she said. "You're not really a Herr Hauptman, are you? The manager was just calling you that to be polite, wasn't he? You're just a lieutenant. You should be a Hauptman though, shouldn't you? You're very handsome, so you should be a Hauptman. That, or even a Herr Major."

Her right hand came up from her side and touched his cheek.

"I'm sorry my fellow country-woman laughed at you. I'd like

to repay you for it. I'd like to make you a Herr Major. Perhaps I can tell you something which will help you to get promotion. I wonder. Just listen to me and then talk to your superiors."

"Talk to them about what?"

Michael watched the boy's face through the mirror and saw it change once more. All the hard arrogance had gone out of it now and it showed a mixture of greed, bewilderment and desire.

"This, just this." Her hand drew away from his face and hung motionless in front of him. "Tell them that in the cause of duty you got—this." Her hand moved still further back and then came forward quickly with the fingers spread like scissors. "Get the driver, Mike," she screamed, as her filed nails went to his eyes in a perfect Chinese uppercut.

Michael moved fast. He swung his chained hands at the driver and felt them go home exactly where he wanted, just below the Adam's apple. At the same instant the handcuffs tightened. He fought against the pain as they bit into his wrists like a rat trap, and grabbing the wheel forced the car across the road to the welcoming light of a tube station.

CHAPTER SEVEN

The Minister's secretary stood five foot six in his shoes and wore double lensed glasses and a rubber corset. These disadvantages appeared to have given him a high opinion of himself, and with his legs astride and hands clasped behind his back, he scowled at Kirk like an irate headmaster.

"No, General, I'm sorry, but the Minister is not pleased, not pleased at all. With the easing of political tension, it takes a lot of work for us to justify this department to the Treasury, and I really cannot think this business is anything more than a wild goose chase. Even if what you tell me is true, what is the importance of this fellow Glyde? The war is over. Haven't you heard that? Besides, the management of the whole affair, or rather the mismanagement, has been most deplorable. I'm not blaming you personally, General Kirk, or you, Mrs. Wise, though it is unprecedented for you as an outsider to have been brought into the department, but—" He threw a look of detestation at Michael. "For one of your staff to go blundering into East Berlin, getting mixed up in a stabbing and escaping after a brawl with the police. Well, as I told the Minister, I consider it to be quite outrageous." He took a loud silk handkerchief out of his pocket and mopped his forehead. "Phew, it's hot in here. Do you mind? He moved to the tightly closed window and started to fiddle with the catch.

"Just—leave—that—alone."

Since he had started his tirade, Kirk had seemed almost oblivious of him. He had lolled back in his chair with his eyes half closed and his thoughts far away, like an oversized dog bothered by a puppy. This sudden threat to his precious warmth brought him to his feet with a jerk, his face scarlet and his hand banging on the table. For a second Penny thought him in danger of apoplexy.

"Yes, I do mind, Mr. Adam Kirsop Vickers, I mind very much, both your criticism of the fitments of my office and of the actions of my staff. Now, just sit down in that chair and listen to me you—you puffed-up schoolboy. Thank you, that's much better. I shall now tell you something for your own good, Mr. Vickers. Firstly, no Minister's secretary, however well connected, is going to come in here and criticise my staff. Any criticism of this department will be directed at me and at me alone. If any head is going to fall it will be mine. Do you want that? If you do, try and get it. Just try and get my head, Mr. Vickers. I wish you luck. Governments change and so do under-secretaries, but I've sat in this office for twenty years, so just try and get my head, if you think you can. Finally, as long as I remain here, I and I alone control this department, answerable only to the Minister in power. Got that, Mr. Vickers?"

"Yes, yes, I'm sorry, perhaps I did speak out of turn." Vickers seemed almost about to burst into tears and his tight suit was suddenly too big for him.

"Good, then let's get on with it." Kirk sat down again and his voice was once more gentle and mild. He was just a courteous old gentleman talking to friends. Out of the corner of his eye he gave a quick wink at Penny.

"When I first took up this assignment, it is possible you might have been right. I may have been on something which was the business of the regular police. I may have been on a wild goose chase. John Glyde may have had an exaggerated personal significance to me. All that might well have been true. But not now, not now, Mr. Vickers, because five people have died. Five people have died because I was right. They have died because I was interested in the life and probable death of Glyde. They were killed because of just that, just that one little personal fact. That makes me right. And this I also know. Because of my interest, somewhere, somebody, something is beginning to fear. It is beginning to get frightened because it has something very terrible to conceal, and it knows I am after it. I know nothing concrete, nothing at all, but I have a notion that the reality may probably surpass your worst imaginings. Tell me, Mr. Vickers. During his trip to Berlin, of which you so much disapprove, my colleague was told abaut a certain Dr. Erich Rhine. Have you any idea, Mr. Vickers, who Dr. Rhine was?"

"No, I'm sorry, General Kirk." Vickers was suddenly completely chastened. "I'm sorry, the name conveys nothing. Nothing at all."

For a moment Kirk didn't go on. He looked at him and there was a slight smile on his heavy face. It had nothing to do with humour.

"No, you wouldn't know. It was an unfair question, let me ask you another. Tell me something else, Mr. Vickers; if you were detailed to arrange the assassination of an important political figure, how would you go about it?"

"I, well really, General, I don't know." He suddenly blushed deeply. "I suppose the first step would be to find the right agent. A hired killer, perhaps. Possibly a fanatic; if you like, a patriot."

"Not bad, not bad at all, Mr. Vickers. Not the hired killer, though. He doesn't exist except in a certain kind of fiction. Believe me, it is just fiction. You see, a hired killer wants to enjoy his hire. He is not going to risk certain death for whatever you offer him. A knife in the alley for some obscure and unimportant victim, but never the big stuff. No, Mr. Vickers, what we want is your second suggestion, the fanatic. All the most successful assassins of history have belonged to that class. Charlotte Corday, Princeps at Sarajevo, Vlada Georgiev who murdered the King of Yugoslavia; all fanatics, all dedicated people. Tell me, my friend, where will you find such an agent?"

"I don't know. They must exist, I suppose."

"Oh yes, they exist, the fanatic exists, but rarely. They are difficult to find. That is why over the last fifty years there have been less cases of major political murder than the fingers on your—no, on my hands." He grinned ruefully at the torn talon on his left arm. "Yes, they are difficult to find. But I wonder, I wonder if there are places where they may be more numerous than others. Places where the fanatic, the dedicated man would be found willing to die for a cause."

"Then you mean?"

"I mean nothing, Mr. Vickers. I just wonder and look at the facts I have, nothing more." He got up from his desk and for the third time that morning bent over the fire.

"You see, we know a little now. We know that Vanek was murdered by a maniac. We know that I was attacked by a woman who had been subjected to a great deal of mental pressure. We know that Glyde was treated for paralysis and possible insanity by a certain Dr. Rhine. This morning I had a long letter from the West German Counter Intelligence Organisation. I now know who Dr. Rhine was."

He moved back to the desk and looked at a long typescript before him, then he sat down and his words were low and quiet.

"People are good, Mr. Vickers. That is, on the whole they are more good than evil. There are certain acts that even the worst of us will not consider. Until. Until certain pressures arise which release something inside me. At times that may happen to a whole nation. I blame nobody. The last war was probably the last. I don't think those pressures will ever trouble us again.

"The fact remains, however, that when Germany was beaten, certain people would not face that defeat as fact. They looked for every means to prolong the struggle. Any means, however vile. Dr. Rhine was part of that means. Here, read it for yourself." He pushed the papers across to Vickers.

For a long time there was silence in the room, broken only by the ticking of the clock and the rustle of the papers as Vickers turned them. At last he threw them down and stood up. His face was very drawn and all the pomposity had left him.

"So that was it," he said, "that was it. The attempted assassination of all the Allied leaders, and by those methods."

"Yes, it's nice reading, isn't it. Very nice. Very nice and tidy and quite logical. As I said, to make that kind of thing work, you need the right agent. The fanatic who will kill and not fear death; who will kill for a cause for righteousness, for the mere sake of killing. Who will risk everything for the sake of the act. Where will we find such an agent?

"Yes, Mr. Vickers, in an asylum. You will find him there. You will take picked cases. They started with religious mania. You take those cases and you pander to them. You agree with their obsessions, and later direct them. With your help, Anti-Christ becomes real. You give them faces to hate and names. Churchill's perhaps or Roosevelt's. And at the end when your work is finished, you give them a gun."

"And that was what happened at Herford."

"That is what should have happened. This Dr. Rhine was put in charge of the Government Research Establishment. He was able to select a number of psychopaths for his experiments. Fortunately the building was bombed and Rhine and his subjects were killed. Two men got away. One of them was this chap Vanek whom Mr. Howard saw in Berlin; the other was John Glyde.

"That is all we know up to date. We don't know yet what was Glyde's actual capacity in that experimental station. Remember Vanek was drunk when he talked to Mr. Howard. He said that Glyde was suffering from paralysis and that certain things were done to him, but he did not state the nature of those things. All he definitely told us was that Glyde got away after the bombing and he mentioned a U-Boat. That is all we know so far, Mr. Vickers."

He broke off for a moment and lifted the ringing telephone beside him.

"Hullo, yes, this is Kirk. Oh, it's you, Inspector. What! Three dead, you say. At Tynecastle. Right. The same hospital, too. Hold on while I take it down. Now, give me the full details."

For perhaps five minutes, Kirk's pencil travelled over the paper; it shook slightly from time to time.

"Now listen to me, Inspector," he said. You've got to get those two men. That's vital. You must take them alive. I know they're armed, but unless we get at least one of them alive, we may later have a bloodbath on our hands. Yes, yes, I was half expecting something of the kind. Yes, I think it had to break. No Inspector, it's not a coincidence, it's too close to the others, Thoday and Hill. It can't be anything else. Now, before you ring off, I want you to do one more thing for me. I have somebody here who is interested in this. Please repeat to him exactly what you have told me."

He smiled his crooked smile at Vickers and handed him the phone.

"Earlier on, Mr. Vickers," he said, "I think I told you this business might well surpass our worst imaginings. It seems that I was right. What has gone before was merely the Overture, now comes the full Opera.

Young George Hamble, the night duty officer, pulled his M.G. into the hospital car park at exactly seven-thirty. There was no need for it, he was not on till eight, but he always liked it that way. It was funny really, he had been a house surgeon at the West Tynecastle Mental Infirmary for over a year now, yet, each time he walked up the steps to the staff entrance he felt a vague sense of excitement and homecoming.

And it was his home. He loved everything about the place and about his work. In particular he loved the night shift. His student days and the holiday factory work still made him think of it as a shift. He loved the nurses and his fellow doctors and the building, with its smell of antiseptic and long, white, corridors. And the patients: above all the patients. He felt strangely like a father to them, for he seemed to understand them so well. He understood their griefs, their fears, their hatreds. There was not one who had been admitted more than a few hours whose name he didn't know, whom he hadn't spoken to, whose illness he hadn't tried to gauge. He was a born healer, a little Geordie crusader for health, with sickness his Saladin.

He hung up his coat, and dressing with care in the white uniform of his calling, walked out of the cloakroom into the long passage that led to "Observation".

"Evenin', Doctor, early again, just can't keep away from the old place, can you? What are you on tonight?"

"Hullo, Bill, yes, I like to keep on time." Hamble grinned at

Bill Stephens, the General Call Orderly, who had chivvied him unmercifully as a student. "Observation again tonight. I'm afraid."

"Pity, Doctor, you'll miss the concert, should be good. They've got that conjuror fellow on the television, I hear. What room are you in, sir? Three. That's those two shock cases, Rodgers and White, isn't it? Well, I'll be seeing you later on, I expect."

"Too right, you will. I want my tea in an hour. There won't be anything doing tonight, I should think. The last injection would have been half an hour ago. No chance of a coma till the morning. I'll ring if I want you, though. Goodnight for the present, Bill."

"Goodnight, sir." Stephens watched him walk quickly down the corridor, his vivid red hair shining under the neon tubes, and he smiled paternally.

"A nice boy," he thought. "A nice, easy, confident way with him, in time he'll make a fine doctor."

At the end of the passage, Hamble paused and looked at his watch. "Ten minutes to go. Plenty of time to take a quick look round the concert hall." He turned off towards the low hum of conversation on the right.

The hall was modern and bright with concealed lighting. It had white bent wood chairs and there were flowers along the parapet of the stage, and a radiogram playing dance music in the corner. The patients sat in long rows, broken here and there by the white coat of a doctor or nurse. Mostly their faces showed only eager expectancy for the show to begin, and the promised appearance of the television star from London. Mostly. Occasionally there was something different. Sad faces, sullen faces, faces that couldn't keep still but twitched and flickered convulsively. Faces to which the name of face was just a word. Masks of flesh, closed without meaning or purpose, staring ahead through eyes in which the light had gone out.

Hamble moved slowly round the aisles. At every row he stopped with a wave and a word for somebody. Nothing he said mattered. He shouted greetings. He cracked pointless jokes. He made platitudes. But he was so good at it. He knew them all by name, he had a smile for all of them, he loved them so much.

He was such a wonder, such a healer, such a Messiah of all hurt, twisted minds that here and there a flicker of hope and answering joy came into this and that tortured face as he passed.

He didn't stay long, it was two minutes to eight as he passed the last row, patting the shoulder of a would-be suicide they had dragged out of Tyne Dock three weeks ago and walked quickly to the Reception Wards, a great glowing warmth inside him from this or that sad, nervous echo of a smile he had managed to raise.

"Hullo, young George. Only just on time tonight, thought I could always count on you being half a hour early." Dr. Grace got up from behind a white cot and took off his glasses.

"Sorry, Doctor, I had a quick look around the concert crowd before I came along."

"Oh, yes, the concert, should be all right, might take a look myself. By the way, how did the game go this afternoon? Getting your handicap down slowly?"

"Very slowly, I'm afraid, sir. Good fun, though, the turf was in lovely condition."

"Glad to hear it, should be considering the money we have to pay that blasted greenkeeper. Must try and get up more often myself, before this really catches me out." He gave a resounding smack to his stomach, and turned to the charts on the wall.

"Well, I'll be getting along now. There's nothing for you to worry about here, I think. They had their last injection at seven. Can't possibly approach their coma stages for six hours, sleeping like babies, both of them. Anyway, keep an eye on them and call as soon as you see any signs of it starting. My word, I'm an old hand at the game, George, but this insulin treatment still gives me the creeps. Just don't know what the blighters are thinking about while they're in it. Well, goodnight, son, and call me if anything happens. Reade will probably look in from time to time."

"Goodnight, sir." Hamble grinned at the large, departing back and turned to the occupants of the two cots.

They were both young, both boys, really, and thank God both caught in time. Both caught with their little agonies of anxiety neurosis while there was still a chance of doing something about it before it turned into a killer.

He looked at each quiet sleeping face and like Grace it gave him the creeps. They weren't there at all. They were never there with insulin. It was as if the person walked away from the world and for a time was somewhere else. First, the early slight injections, the confusion, the fighting against them. Then the sweating as the doses increased and the sugar slowly left the blood stream, and this present sleep followed. Finally, the watching stage, the change as the mind slipped from sleep to coma, and in coma tried to dream of its past and the thing that troubled it and which lasted for perhaps half an hour before the quick, urgent tube of glucose saved the body from death. He looked at the charts and the notes above the bed. Everything in order. Rodgers thirty-seven courses, White thirty-two. Temperatures normal for the treatment. Four and five under. Pulse six and seven under. The faces blank and restful. The conflict, if it was a conflict, buried and hidden, in another world.

"Yes," said Hamble, who was a great reader and knew his Alice. "Yes, there is another shore, you know, upon the other side." He leaned over, checked the pressure gauges and the thermometers and then went back to the desk and made notes on each chart.

For two hours he had a quiet time. The patients slept. The night orderly brought him tea. Once Dr. Reade came in for two minutes and glanced at the charts. Everything was as it should be. From time to time he could hear a murmur of laughter from the concert hall and the snatch of a popular song.

It was nine o'clock before he noticed that there was something wrong. It was nothing definite. The dials showed the same reading as they had done before, the breathing was regular, there was no hint of the approach of coma. But as he looked over Rodgers's face he knew it was wrong, for he was no longer sleeping.

Hamble peered at him. There was still nothing out of order. Nothing he had been warned about, told to watch for. The eyes were still shut, the breathing was steady, but in the face there was an expression he had never seen in sleep. It was firm, steady and purposeful, and it seemed to be watching him through those tightly shut eyes.

He glanced at the gauges, dreading a drop in the readings which would tell him that the crisis was premature, that the coma had begun too soon and send him rushing for the glucose syringe and Grace's bell, and as he looked, the pulse reading began to rise. It rose quickly but falteringly like a tired, still muscular arm, till it showed two points above that of a normal human being in good health, and with it the temperature changed too. There was no hint of coma, no crisis. After four days of insulin, four days without sugar, in contradiction of every known medical precept, Rodgers was coming back.

He stared over the boy's face, unbelieving, doubting, thinking the readings must be false, and knew they were right as Rodgers opened his eyes. He opened them wide as if he had just come out of a light and easy sleep, and he stared at Hamble. He didn't seem to like what he saw. His lips drew back in a snarl and there was a flicker of hatred in the tired eyes.

"So it was you! " he said. "I know who you are. I know you because your—your—your—"

Hamble bent his head lower desperately listening for the word from those faltering lips, and then turned and dashed for the bell. He almost reached it when the room went dark.

CHAPTER EIGHT

The terrace was so battered, so decayed, so past repair that no one had bothered to fill the bomb gash that separated the end house from the rest of the row.

Now it stood derelict and indecent in the glare of the searchlight, all its scars made plain, like an elderly, sagging strip-tease artiste on a fairground stage. In front of it was the tall railway embankment and behind a slope of rubble, ash, rusty tins and dispirited grass led down to the river.

Kirk and Michael walked along the cobbles through the thin half drizzle, half mist, from the sea and turned under the arch where the first police squad was stationed. They had been motoring for over six hours and they were very tired with faces like items in an antiquarian bookseller's catalogue. Original binding, grey boards, slightly dust-marked.

The Inspector stood a few yards to the side of the searchlight and he just managed to raise a smile.

"Ah, there you are, sir, and you, Mr. Howard, glad you made it, but I'm afraid you're just in time for the kill. You know Dr. Grace and Dr. Reade, don't you?"

"Of course I do." Kirk held out his hand. "Bad business, I'm afraid."

Reade nodded. She wore an old raincoat and fur boots, and her homely, warm face gave a slight air of comfort to the depressing scene, but Grace stuttered badly and his hand shook.

"Yes, yes, very bad," he said. "But thank God you're here, General Kirk, because you've got to stop them. We've got to know what happened, you see. It's my fault, it has to be my fault, but all the same you must stop them." All the bounce had left him and his suit seemed too big for him, he was like a pupa that had died in his cocoon.

"You see, something went wrong with the treatment. I don't know what, because at the moment it seems impossible, but it has to be that, it can't be anything else, General, these men, the one man that's left, he isn't a criminal. He isn't responsible for what he is doing, for his actions, so you must stop them. If they put the tear gas in, it will be just plain murder."

"Tear gas, I see." Kirk turned to the inspector. "Just in time for the kill, I think you said, old boy. Now listen to me. I know this is a wretched business, but before you start anything, please give me a rough resumé of what has actually happened. Remember that apart from your phone call, I'm completely in the dark."

"Three of them, General. Three of our boys shot down in cold blood, unarmed, and he calls it murder." The Inspector threw a look of detestation at Grace. "No, I'm sorry, General, but this thing has gone far enough. I've got permission from my superiors now, and as soon as the gas gets here; we had to send to Edinburgh for it, I'm putting it in. After that, if he doesn't come out with his hands up, then we shoot to kill."

"Easy, old boy, just take it easy. You're probably right, but just take it easy. Excuse me a minute."

He reached in his pocket and pulled a cigar from his case. He put it in his mouth but didn't light it at once. He smiled at the policeman and then strolled forward to the mouth of the archway, looking out at the floodlit house and the loom of the four tall bridges behind it. From the east bend of the river there was a faint trickle of dawn beginning to creep over the town. He took out his matches and slowly struck one. At the first flicker of light there was an answering gleam from the house, a faint report and the whine of a bullet striking the wall beside him.

He lit his cigar with care, grinned and then walked back to the group round the searchlight.

"Yes, Inspector," he said. "I see your point. Still, I'd like to know a little more, if I may. Just tell me what happened."

"We haven't got the early details exactly, sir. The doctor on night duty has only just come round and the orderly is in no condition to talk. All we know is that when these two men were in this sleep treatment, they woke up. They should have been right out, approaching a coma, yet they woke up. There was a young doctor in the room with them. He spotted there was something wrong, and bent over one of them. The patient tried to say something to him but seemed too weak, so he went to the bell to call Dr. Grace here. He appears to have been struck on the head from behind just before he got to it. That's all he could tell us. As I said, the orderly is still out. We found him lying in the passage; he'd been beaten up badly. May even die."

"I see, Inspector. You know I'd give a great deal to hear what that patient was trying to say. I wouldn't be surprised if it wasn't the key to the whole business. Please go on, Inspector."

"Well, then they came out of the ward, sir. They took some clothes from the staff room and stole a car from outside the hospital. We were informed of all this at exactly nine thirty-five. It was just after that we phoned you, sir, as you instructed."

"You did quite right. Go, on, old boy."

"The next thing that happened was that we got a report about a gunsmith's shop in Westland Row being broken into. The squad car was sent round and then we got the first killing. The sergeant went to the door and was shot down. The men put five bullets into him. Any of them would have proved fatal. Our driver kept his head. He followed them on the car, keeping down all the time while the one in the back tried to shoot at him. He fired at least five rounds. The driver kept his radio on and gave us a commentary of what happened. Well, sir, he tried to ram them at the corner here.

He got the car, but they got him. That's the lot. We've surrounded the house. Thank God it was empty. We evacuated all the terrace. They killed another officer while we were doing just that. No, sir, three dead and I'm not playing any more. In ten minutes I expect to get the gas cylinders and then we're going in,"

"And I'm sure you're right. I don't blame you at all. Ten minutes before the cylinders, I think you said. That gives me time. But I understand there was only one man now."

"Yes, sir." The Inspector looked suddenly embarrassed. "We got one. He came out firing. We had to, sir. We had to protect ourselves."

"Of course you did, old boy. Of course you did. Now just switch off your light for a moment because I'm going into that house, and I don't want any glare. Ten minutes I think you said."

"Yes, sir, about that. But may I ask just what you intend?"

"No, boy, you may not. All I can tell you is what I did the first time when I asked you to let me know about any out of the way occurrence connected with mental cases in this area. You did that and I am grateful, now I take over." He pulled his coat a little tighter around him and turned to Reade.

"Tell me, doctor," he said. "This treatment, the insulin. I have read a little about it, not much, but as I understand it, the coma lasts at the outside about forty-five minutes. These two men, Rodgers and White, when this thing happened, they were about to approach the coma, I think. What I want to know is this. The physical state at the time of awakening, what would it be?"

She turned and looked towards the house and there was no longer any comfort in her calm, level voice.

"Sorry, General. I'm very sorry, but I just don't know. The thing seems impossible. You see we drive out the sugar. The insulin drives it out of the blood stream. That's what causes the weakness, the final coma. The idea is that in the weakness the mind becomes empty, ready for self adjustment, a void in which adjustment may come. The body at the end is terribly weak. Forty-five minutes is the maximum we can keep up the coma, after that comes death. That is why this is all impossible. Unless." Her expression changed for a moment and then she looked away from him.

"Yes, Dr. Reade, unless something happened. Unless in that void, not adjustment but something else came in. Something from outside perhaps. Could it have been that, do you think? That's what we have to find out now. Tell me one more thing, doctor. If that man in there woke up now, shook off whatever is controlling him, what would he do?"

"He would die, that is quite definite." She was very confident in her statement. "I don't know what is keeping him alive now. Whatever it is, it follows no normal laws. You see, his body is burnt up. The energy has gone. He should have died hours ago. All the time we have to be very careful during this treatment. During the coma stage we have to watch every symptom, and once the crisis is reached, sugar must be injected at once, neat glucose. That man has had no sugar for over eight hours. As I said, I don't know what is keeping him up, but remove it, and he'll die at once. I'm terribly sorry to say this, but I think you're wasting your time, General Kirk. You too, doctor." Her hand touched his arm for a moment. "There's nothing anybody can do for him any more, except stop further violence. I'm afraid you'll have to go ahead with your tear gas, Inspector."

"Thank you, Marm, that's just what I intend to do. I fancy this is it now." He pointed to the black car that was coming, without lights, from the far end of the tunnel.

"Remember, Inspector. Ten minutes you said." Kirk glanced at his watch. "I've still six left. Six minutes to play it my way."

"Very good, sir. You have your six minutes. I was told to co-operate with you. Do what you want." He looked away from him at the small green cylinders like outsize pepper pots they were handing out of the car. "Have it your way, though personally I think we'll have to sweep you up with a broom when all this is over."

"Perhaps you will have to, Inspector, perhaps you will. If so, please accept my thanks in advance for that last service." He pulled his hat down tighter on his head and began to walk forward.

"No, sir, you can't do it that way. It's far too big a risk. Ten to one at least that he'll shoot." Michael stepped in front of him. "If you must go, let's take it together. We'll have a better chance that way."

"Inspector Jackson." Kirk wheeled round like a pivot. "You

have been given orders to co-operate with my department. If this man interferes any further, you are to place him under arrest. Now switch off your light. Get out of my way, Mike." He walked quickly out to the mouth of the tunnel.

As the searchlight went out, noise seemed to increase. The slightest sounds began to grow and multiply and become suddenly significant. The thud of his shoes on the steaming cobbles, the whirr of a distant express running north, the rattle behind him as the police adjusted the gas bombs.

From a tenement window to the left, a woman started to sing. It was a cheap, hackneyed song, and her voice was thick and tuneless, but to him it suddenly seemed immensely sad and haunting and important. The last thing he might ever hear in his life.

SWEET ROSY O'GRADY, SHE'S MY LOVELY ROSE.

At any moment it might stop. There would be a flicker of light from the window of that darkened house and everything would stop for ever. The sodden dawn would close up in a flash of pain, and he would never know the end of the story. In front of him he could see the sun climbing wearily up from beyond the river. It was a pale watery sun, but how he wished it would stay—

SHE'S MY LOVELY LADY—

"A hundred yards to the door now. Just a hundred little yards across the cobbles. One, two, three—ninety yards. Hang on, whoever you are behind the window. Hang on, Rodgers, White, whatever your name is, because I'm coming to help you. No, not you. It's not you I want, but the thing behind you, so just cry and fight it and don't shoot. Look at me, hate me, spit at me, but please, please don't shoot. Twenty-seven, twenty-eight, twenty-nine. Seventy yards to go."

MOST EVERYONE KNOWS.

"That's right, sing, you hag, keep on singing, you beery old bitch with a mouth like flannel. Do anything else you like, rob a church, beat your child, but just keep on singing."

AND SOON WE'LL BE MARRIED? OH HOW HAPPY WE'LL BE.

"If he's going to fire he'll have to fire soon. Forty yards to go, just forty little yards. Take it easy. Walk slowly and confidently, and don't let him see you're frightened. But you're not, are you? Not frightened of dying, not of going out. Just of leaving everything: your office, the telephone, your stuffy flat in South Ken. Leaving and never knowing the end of the story, that's all you're frightened about. Twenty to go. Stop here and flick the ash from your cigar. That's it, nice and easy. Let him look at you. All right, boy, I'm coming in now."

FOR I LOVE SWEET ROSY O'GRADY, AND ROSY O'GRADY LOVES ME.

The song died away and as its echo, a steamer hooted far down the river. Through the corner of his eye, Kirk saw something move in the window. He forced himself to ignore it, and the next moment his hand was on the knob of the crazy battered door.

It opened easily, dragging along the floor on sagging hinges, and he stepped up into the dark room. It smelt of dust, wood rot, and incongruously of antiseptic. It was the boy who smelt of that. The boy stood, leaned rather, against the wall by the window and he had a rifle in his hands. He looked towards Kirk and the rifle came up very slowly. It wasn't as if he was holding it at all but that the rifle itself was rising and lifting him with it. He had a pale, freckled, rather pleasant face and it was completely without expression. He didn't seem to see Kirk at all.

Kirk took the cigar out of his mouth and he smiled at him.

"Hullo, son," he said. "You can put it down now, I think. It's all over now and we're going home." He started to walk towards him and his heavy, tired face was very full of understanding. He was complete security, the loving father, the eternal Dad.

He saw the arm holding the gun stiffen, the finger go white on the trigger, but he didn't hurry. Very gently his maimed hand reached for the gun barrel and turned it away from him. Then he grasped the boy's arm and pulled him towards him.

"Wake up, son," he said. "Just wake up and tell me about it. He looked into the weak face and saw something change. "Just tell me why you did it."

"It was the doctor, he had, he had—" The face struggled with the gigantic effort of speech.

"Go on, son. Go on, what was it that the doctor had?"

"He had—," he leaned forward towards Kirk, and he hadn't much farther to go. "He had red hair."

The body suddenly went stiff and at the same instant Kirk felt the pulse stop.

CHAPTER NINE

Penny turned her Riley into the Park, missing other vehicles by inches. Half her concentration was on the traffic and half on Michael.

"And you think he may just possibly have been on that U-Boat?"

"We can't even guess that yet. We got this message from the German Admiralty last night, they've been really most co-operative. You remember Paul Vanek mentioned something about putting your brother on a U-Boat. Yes, well, he may have been telling the truth. There was one based at Bergen Fiord that fits. She was a small coastal type with short range and her fuel tanks were only half full. On May the first, forty-five, a military aeroplane flew into Bergen from Germany. A passenger was put on the submarine, the U.1760, and he was said to have taken something with him. We don't know what, but it was something bulky. The U-Boat sailed that night under sealed orders and she never came back.

"Our first thought was that she might have been trying to make a neutral port. Spain for example or South America, but it won't fit. A short range type with half empty tanks would never have made it. She might have had a rendezvous with another vessel, but it seems unlikely. Look out!"

"Orl rite." Amid a screaming of horns and tyres, Penny pulled round the artillery memorial and shooting across the bows of two purple-faced bus drivers turned into the Park.

"And now this old brute of an admiral is putting his oar in."

"He most certainly is. We rang him up this morning and asked for his co-operation. Not a bit of it unless he gets a full and detailed account of our reasons for the enquiry. Then it will be checked and double checked by the proper quarters in Naval Intelligence, considered by himself and if he then thinks it a right and proper course of action, he may be good enough to help."

"What's Kirk done about that?"

"Only thing he could. Gone over the old devil's head to the First Sea Lord. Our friend will have to do what he's told now, but I can't say I relish the interview."

"Poor darling." She took her hand off the wheel and stroked his cheek as they rounded the Palace Fountain. "What did you say his name was?"

"Admiral the Honourable Sir Fetherstone-Chadwick-Vane, may hell be hot for him. Why are you laughing?"

"Because it's damned funny. I know all about him. He's a terror. His secretary runs a yacht club I used to go to. Silly little bastard called Jimmy Hicks, Lieutenant Commander. Calls himself Commodore at the club. Well, here we are, Sweet." She pulled the car across the Mall to the Citadel entrance. "Tear a strip off old Vane for me and give Jimmy my love. I don't think he loves me much, I took some of the car boys down to the club and they got a bit high." Her hand reached for his for a second. "Ring me when you can. Promise."

"Yes, I promise. Soon as I can." He smiled, got out and walked across the pavement to the frowning, concrete lair of the dragon.

As Penny had said, Lieutenant Commander Hicks was a silly little bastard. He ran down the steps of the Citadel entrance to Michael and he was just too jaunty, too well pressed, too much the stage picture of the breezy nautical man. At any moment Michael felt he would burst into song.

"Oh, I'm the Captain of the Pinafore," he would begin and Michael in his toneless bass would be forced to reply.

"And a right good captain too."

Mercifully he didn't. He shook Michael's hand in a grip that was too firm and manly and led him into the crowded passages of the building, chattering as he went.

"Well, I must say I'm glad you're punctual, Mr. Howard. The old boy's in a hell of a flap. Doesn't like it a bit, your going over his head to the First Lord. Not used to it, you know. Not used to it at all. Been taking it out of me all morning."

"Sorry about that, Commander, by the way, I believe we have a mutual friend, a Mrs. Wise."

"Oh yes, Penny. Grand lass, used to come down to the club quite often last season. The North Dorset Yacht Club, that is. As a matter of fact, I'm the Commodore." He glowed with pride, and no yachts, but a dozen grey battleships seemed to swim behind his eyes.

" 'Fraid I had to rather tear a strip off poor old Penny recently. She brought some dreadful types down with her. People connected with the motor industry, I believe. Not at all our sort." He halted before an unnumbered green door.

"Well, here we are, Howard. The sanctum. Go easy with him for my sake. His bark is said to be worse than his bite, but I'm not sure I believe that." He knocked timidly at the door, winced at an answering growl from within and pushed it open.

Admiral the Hon. Fetherstone-Chadwick-Vane had two faces. His own, which was normally keen and breezy, and the other morose, glowering and hostile, modelled on his boyhood hero, Lord Fisher.

At the moment Fisher was very much in evidence. Heavy, flushed, thick lips drawn down, eyes slitted in his scowl, a brooding, irascible, Negroid Beethoven, he looked with loathing at Michael.

"Good afternoon, Mister Mik—el How—ard." Without difficulty he made each syllable vaguely insulting. "So you're the young man who's been annoying me, are you. The young man who kept bothering me for certain of our files and then went above my head to the First Lord."

"Not personally, sir. It was my superior, General Kirk."

"Kirk, eh. General as well. Disgraceful. Risen to quite a decent military rank in his disreputable profession. Pity he didn't pick up a few manners to go with it. No, sir. He asked for these files. I gave him a perfectly civil reply that they would be examined by the proper department of Naval Intelligence and in the course of time the details would probably be passed on to him. Not content with that he goes telling tales above my head and I get this."

His hand came down with a crash at the heavily embossed sheet of paper in front of him.

"Well, I'm in your hands now, it seems. This orders me to co-operate with your department to the fullest extent. I obey my orders and you shall have your co-operation, but I still feel it's most uncommonly uncivil. Why couldn't this feller Kirk come to me like a Christian? Have a yarn about it, tell me what it was all about, instead of running to those nincompoops of politicians."

"I'm sorry, sir." Michael really did feel slightly sorry for this injured Neptune. "The fact is, this business is top secret and time is all important."

"Time—important." Vane snorted. "First I've heard of that in a government office. Extraordinary thing. Well, now you're here let's get down to business as you call it. Hicks!"

"Sir!" Hicks leapt to attention and slightly raised his voice.

"Don't shout at me like that, Lieutenant Commander, just get those papers we sorted out." He rubbed the side of his purple face. "Bawling in me ear like that. Nobody seems to have any manners these days. Learn them in your wretched yacht club, I expect. Do you sail, Mr. Howard?"

"No, no, sir, I'm afraid not."

"Don't be afraid. No need to be. One slight thing in your favour. Lot of grown men mucking about in miserable little boats on a sour canal. Calling themselves by naval ranks they're not entitled to. Common chaps as well, some of them. Shopkeepers, house agents, that class of feller. Women, too, footlin' about half nude. Makes me sick."

He turned again like a blight on the unfortunate Hicks.

"Well, don't just stand there, man, jawing all day about your wretched hobby. Give me the papers."

"At once, sir." Hicks spread a chart and a pile of buff-coloured foolscap on the desk.

"Right, let's get down to it, shall we?" He glanced at the top sheet and then looked up at Michael, "just a minute, though, your name, Howard, rings a bell. Any relation to a Captain Howard? Old Hippo Howard?"

In far-off memory Michael recalled a childhood visit to an enormous, ill-tempered relative with a game leg who could easily have answered to Hippo. "Yes, sir," he said. "My great-uncle."

"Well, you don't say. Should have told me at once. Saved a lot of bad feeling." Lord Fisher's hostile face seemed to shrink slightly and Vane's own features appeared. "Wonderful chap, Hippo. Ever tell you how he crocked his leg?"

He had done in great detail, but Michael thought it policy to shake his head.

"No. Well, he was on *Athene* in the South Atlantic. 'Sixteen, I think it was. Wretched little single-screw light cruiser, escort to three tramps. Along comes a bloody great Hun armoured cruiser. Choice with Hippo. He's got three knots advantage, so what should he do. Run or fight. Not bound to fight, yer know, with those odds against you. Well, he did fight. Strung up his best hoist of flags and went for her. Crocked his leg, lost *Athene* and half his crew, but the merchantmen got away. This is the joke, though. The ruddy signal he flew. Know what it was? "England expects too bloody much." He shook with laughter and then turned to the desk again.

"Well, this won't do." Once more Lord Fisher took over.

"You want to know what happened to a U-Boat that left Bergen fiord on the evening of May first, nineteen forty-five. You were told about this from the German records, but you can't or won't let me know what is important about it." He flipped over the second sheet of paper. "I can do better. I know where she is." Like a showman producing the big act he pushed a reel of film to Michael.

The picture was very dark and indistinct. It showed a coast-line on a misty day. There were hills in the background and the hint of a lake behind the shore. In the centre of the picture there was a small point like a rock in the water. Michael flicked through the reel. Nothing moved except the point. It seemed to rise slowly and there was a huge white spray to the side of it. Then its shape changed, it rose forward and was no longer a point, but a long cigar reaching out of the water. That was all.

"That's exhibit one. Very bad photography, I'm afraid, but we never managed to tear a strip off the poor devil who took it. Didn't get it for nine months afterwards. Came from a coastal command Sunderland. She was returning to her base at Ullapool, that's in Ross and Cromarty, from an Iceland convoy patrol. All very routine. Never got back, though. Found her much later, miles off course on top of a mountain called rather inappropriately Ben Loyal. The crew all appeared to have been killed in the crash, though it was obvious she had been in action. All bombs gone and she was riddled with cannon shells. The only thing we got of interest was that roll of film."

"And you think that this," Michael pointed to the cigar-shape, "This is the U-Boat we want."

"Don't be impertinent, Mr. Howard. I don't think, I wouldn't have wasted your time if I merely thought. No, I'm quite sure. Look at this."

Exhibit two was a blueprint. Except that it showed the hull of a submarine, it was meaningless to Michael.

"Yes, that's her. One of the latest coastal types they put out. Very small displacement, short range, only speed to recommend 'em really. Armed with a type of Oerlikon that used the same shells we found in the Sunderland.

"Now this is the point." He took up another paper. "The boat that left Bergen was of this type. An SL2. From this picture I can tell that the joker we have here was an SL2. The step of the bows is unique. We too have had some slight access to German files, Mr. Howard, and we know that there were only five of this type completed. Two were scuttled at Kiel, one we sunk in the December off the Dogger Bank and one was captured and given to the Russians. That leaves one left. One that is now lying somewhere, anywhere, here." He took up a red pencil and drew a thick line along the chart. It showed the tip of Scotland and stretched from John O'Groats to Cape Wrath.

"Can't go any closer yet, I'm afraid. As I said, the plane was off course. Nobody bothered at the time. From that picture we know the boys got a definite kill and there was no point in looking for remains. Still, we're checking on the coast-line now. Won't take long. Let you know to within a few yards. Probably somewhere near the Kyle of Durness, I shouldn't wonder, though what the hell she was doing there is anybody's guess."

"She may have been dropping something, sir." Michael looked at the deep inlet on the map. It was an ideal place for what he thought might have happened. Still water, deserted coast, a minor road within easy walking distance, a foggy day, and then literally out of the blue came the Sunderland.

"Dropping something, what the devil do you mean? Mines. Not much point up there, no shipping. Besides this SL type weren't fitted as mine layers."

"No, sir, not mines. Something that went ashore—someone

perhaps—" He broke off as the phone rang at the Admiral's elbow.

"Hullo, yes, of course it is. Oh, it's you, is it Miles. 'Bout time too. Got the position for me. Right, let's have it." His heavy hand picked up a pair of compasses and he bent over the chart. "Yes, Spey inlet, eh. I wasn't far out. Five degrees Ben Armin, eighty from the point. Thank you, Miles. Goodbye." He dropped the phone back into the stand and carefully pencilled a light cross on the chart.

"Well, that's that, Mr. Howard. I was only five miles out. The other side of the peninsula. That's what you wanted."

"Not quite, sir, I'm afraid this is just the beginning." Michael glanced at the First Lord's orders and took courage. "You see, it's vitally important that we get the log and papers of that U-Boat. We were hoping that you would attend to that for us." He steeled himself for the coming outburst.

It never came, Vane started to open his mouth in protest and then changed his mind. Perhaps the enormous, peg-legged ghost of Hippo Howard seemed to give his blessing to the enterprise. Instead of rage, Michael was subjected to a long and depressing discourse on the difficulties of salvage operations.

He learned of tides scouring debris high over the sunken object. The inability of divers to work in long stretches. The placing of air pumps and cutters. The deep shelving of the Scottish coast.

"Good grief, man, she's been under twelve years and we don't know where the bomb got her. There's probably not a bulkhead left standing, and twenty feet of mud over her by now. You've only got one slight point in your favour. As far as we know the Jerries always kept their papers in waterproof safes. If that one was secured, there's just a vague chance we might find something. But have you the remotest idea of what this will cost?"

"No, sir, I'm afraid not."

"Neither have I, not the slightest, and I can't say I care." Vane suddenly roared with laughter. "Don't care a bit, besides it'll do those fat bastards at Scapa good to have a bit of exercise. Right, we'll see about getting her up for you. Hicks, what sort of bottom have you got?"

"I beg your pardon, sir." The Lieut. Commander blushed like a girl.

"The sea bottom, you imbecile. What is the geological structure—of the sea bed—at the position I have indicated—on this chart—Commodore." At each pause his hand crashed on the desk.

"I'll find out, sir." Like a caged mouse Hicks scurried to a shelf of reference books in the corner of the room.

"Volcanic ash, sir, some shale and white sand. On the whole clean."

"Good, she shouldn't be silted over then, that's one mercy. The depth should be around twenty fathoms, I imagine."

"No, sir," Hicks spoke from behind his book. "I'm afraid there's a fall. A valley; it hasn't been sounded, but is thought to be between forty and sixty fathoms. The natives call it the Hole of Sunda."

"Thank you, my friend, as always a bringer of cheering news. Sixty, eh. That means twenty minute spells. Good weather now, but just a few nice, big Western Ocean rollers and we've had it, so let's get on with it. What have they got for the job at Scapa, Hicks?"

"There's *Hybrid*, sir, Captain Wollestone. She's just back from a refit."

"*Hybrid*, eh. She'll do. Wake Paddy Wollestone up to have to get cracking with a raw crew. Do the feller a lot of good. Now, you can do some work. Send a signal to Scapa that they are to commence operations at once. Then find out what is the best route to this Place Spey Inlet and book a couple of sleepers on the night train. We'll meet *Hybrid* up there."

"Tonight, sir, but I was hoping, that is I thought. As I told you it's our annual Regatta on Saturday and—"

"And therefore, Commodore, the fleet will have to put to sea without its beloved leader. Tonight, Hicks."

"Yes, sir, of course, sir; one small point though, that signal to Scapa, it is customary to give them a code name."

"Thank you, so it is. What shall it be." He glanced with loathing at the Sea Lord's orders. "Yes, I think we shall call it 'Operation Pressgang.' "

That night it was stifling in London. Heavy, unbreakable clouds moved in from the West and hung like a thick, quilted eiderdown over the town.

In her mews flat, Penny Wise had a final nightcap and went to bed early. She didn't sleep but rolled for hours on the divan, gasping for air and listening to the distant thunder that brought no rain.

She thought about Michael. A long time about Michael. Michael and Kirk and Germany and the hurt minds and the force that directed them. That and her brother. Always her brother. Somewhere he existed in space and time and she had to find him because he was the key to everything. Somewhere. Where? Very slowly an idea was growing in her mind. She pulled herself wearily out of bed and scrawled a note on the memo pad.

At about the same time, a young reporter in a sweltering news office had the same idea. He had just taken down a phone message and for a long time he merely stared at it. Then he crossed to the back files of the month and took a lot of notes. When he had finished he went over to the night editor's office and handed them to him.

"Yes, interesting, could be, just possibly could be." The night editor was a gloomy man with ulcers, usually remote and non-committal. For once he showed a little enthusiasm.

"Yes, this chap tonight makes the eighth nut killing they've had up there in a fortnight. A woman, too. All in the same area, a ten mile radius. Um, interesting. Tell you what, you can drop everything and concentrate on it. Good idea you've got. "An epidemic of insanity strikes town. When will it spread?" Yes, by all means get on with it."

Hicks lay miserably on his berth in the sleeper and watched his superior prepare himself for rest. He took his time about it, washing with care, patting lotion into his cheeks, cleaning his teeth with unnecessary violence and taking a long swig of brandy to protect his chest from the treacherous night air.

Hicks closed his eyes and tried to think of pleasanter things. The Regatta he would miss, the flags bright around the pier, the jokes in the club-house after the races and the blonde divorcee

who was to have been his crew. The Admiral's noisy gargle
brought him back to reality with a jerk.

Through the night the long train creaked and groaned in the
northern cuttings.

CHAPTER TEN

Although the Spey Moor Hotel was small, isolated and unused
to visitors, Admiral Vane had managed to make himself
pretty comfortable. He had half cajoled, half bullied the wretched
manageress to turn over the whole of the first floor to him as a personal suite; bedroom, study, sitting-room, dining-room, and with
the promise of bribes, threats and rank ill-temper was accorded the
respect due to a 'king across the water.' Now he stood morosely by
the Naval Hillman and watched Michael climb out.

"Ah, here you are at last, Howard, foul journey I expect, foul
place here, foul climate, foul people." He stared with fury at the
sodden, rock-strewn moorland, the grey Atlantic swell and the
gaunt housekeeper who was lifting out Michael's bag.

"You'll be good enough to take that up to Mr. Howard's room
now, Mrs. MacDoggart, while we have a drink."

"Aye, sir, of course." She looked at Michael. "I'm afraid it's a
very wee one, sir, one of the servant's rooms; you see, the Admiral has taken all the guest rooms and—"

"Nonsense, woman, very decent little room. Would have
liked it myself if I hadn't needed to be near my office. Very pretty
view of—of the—the chapel. Well, come in out of his drizzle,
Howard, sign the book and we'll partake of a dram together.
That's the one decent thing to be said for the place, they've got
some quite drinkable liqueur whiskey." He stomped up the steps
into the dark hall grumbling as he went.

"Been over a week in this dump already, just about had enough
of it. Better than living on *Hybrid* I suppose, a frigate rigged for
salvage is no place for a Christian. Hicks probably enjoys it,
reminds him of his wretched yacht club I shouldn't wonder. Still
it's tonight or never, thank goodness, one way or the other we
pack up tonight."

"Tonight, sir? I got your signal, but I couldn't quite make out the urgency from your standpoint."

"Couldn't you? Thought it was clear enough. You will, soon as we've had a drink. Sign the book, man, you won't get one if you don't, very law abiding people the aborigines. Here, what's that you've put down." He leaned over Michael's shoulder breathing heavily.

Michael glanced at his scrawl on the damp paper. 'M. G. Howard, London, British.'

"Yes, British, that's it. Why British. Where were you born, up here, Ireland, Wales?"

"I was born in Dover, sir."

"Dover. Dover's in England, isn't it? You're English. Cross it out and write English. No need to hint you may be connected with one of three enslaved and degenerate races. Good, now we can have our drink. Tessie, service."

He bellowed at the aged crone at the bar and glanced with love at the glasses and amber bottle she put before them.

"Well, cheers. Now you were saying that you didn't quite grasp my signal though I thought I'd made it clear enough. Either we get your papers tonight or the *Hybrid* packs up without them and goes back to Scapa."

"But why, sir, what's the urgency?"

"The urgency, Mr. Howard, is that after tonight we can't go on, because in the morning there's going to be a damned big storm and our lines won't stand that. Usually don't trust the Met boys, but now I can smell it."

He sniffed the thick atmosphere of peat smoke, stale spirits and tobacco and refilled his glass.

"Yes, I'm afraid it's tonight or never, as far as this year's concerned, anyway."

"And the chances of getting them tonight?"

"Can't say. Done quite well, so far, found her easily. The bomb had got her six feet from the bow; practically blown it off. We've put an air lock over that and pumped out the first compartment. They should be busy with the second now. If the rest of the ship is watertight, we might have a chance of finding the safe; if not, we haven't got time. Simple as that. I'm going out to *Hybrid* now, care to come after you've had another drink?"

"Thank you, sir, I would like to come very much. Not another drink, though. I'll just slip up and have a wash while you're finishing yours."

"Very well. Your room's right at the top. You can't miss it, very pleasant and airy. I'll lend you an oilskin. It's beginning to blow a bit already."

As Mrs. MacDoggart had said, the room was very wee. Except in the very centre it was impossible to stand upright at all. He bent low and craned out of the window, looking at the tin shack that was the chapel, the dank slope to the sea and the mast of *Hybrid* swaying above the headland on the North Atlantic swell. Somewhere beneath her there might just be the answer to the question. The big question. No longer the punishment of a traitor, but a national crisis.

Somewhere at the bottom of the valley they called the 'Hole of Sunda' he might find where John Glyde had gone. It had to be this way, there was no other. The German reports tied up too closely to be circumstantial. He had come to England. Come here and brought something with him. Now the fruit of that coming was beginning to grow. Already the preface was over and the play had begun. The headlines were right. 'Epidemic of Madness'. 'Mania Incorporated' were yesterday's. During the last week there had been two more outbreaks in the Tyne area and with the headlines, panic was starting. How much longer had they got?

He glanced at his watch. Five hours to midnight, and how long to the morning storm? Already it was coming. There were white flecks on the water and ragged clouds piling in the West.

"Our great, grey mother," the Irish writer had called the sea. "The scrotum tightening sea." James Joyce was dead; dead in Trieste, with "his left eye wake, and its neighbour full of water, Man." But John Glyde and his works were alive, alive and kicking and somewhere in the womb of that grey mother there might be a clue to his actions.

He splashed tepid water from the bowl on the washstand and hurried downstairs as Vane's bellow thundered through the house.

The *Hybrid's* launch was waiting at the end of a ramshackle stone jetty about a hundred and fifty yards from the house. Vane growled at the sailors who helped him on to her lurching deck and sat down heavily in the stern, looking in his oilskins and southwester for all the world like an advertisement for somebody's herrings. He licked a gnarled red finger and held it up into the sodden air.

"No, I don't like it," he said. "Don't like it at all. Blowing up fast in the west. Won't hold till morning, whatever those B.F.s at the Met office say." He pulled himself up in his seat and bawled at the petty officer in charge. "Come on, Coxson, get her moving, or do you expect Mr. Howard and myself to get out and walk on the bloody waters."

"Aye aye, sir. At once, sir. Just waiting to see you were comfortably settled, sir." The man cast off the mooring lines and grinned hugely at Vane. Apparently to the lower deck at least the Admiral was affectionately regarded as a character.

As they rounded the headland the coming storm seemed very close. The white flecks Michael had noticed from the window were enormous and menacing at water level while the ragged clouds were now a long black bar across the whole horizon. Already the wind was blowing up and there were plumes of spray around their oilskins at each corkscrew dip of the boat's prow. Only *Hybrid* herself was still. A grey, light dotted rock in the dusk, with huge cables fore and aft and a tangle of lines and hoses hanging over her side like creepers. It was like coming into another, more peaceful, world as the launch turned into the still water of her lea and came smoothly to a stop alongside the rope ladder.

Michael watched Vane leap for it with surprising agility and pull himself steadily upwards. He followed him with less skill, banging against the side of the frigate at every step and reached the deck on his knees, to be lifted gently to his feet by two grinning ratings.

"Well, here we are, Paddy, in for the kill one way or the other." Vane drew him towards a tall, still youthful officer at his side. "This is the young man who's put us to all the trouble. Mr. Howard, Captain Wollestone."

"How do you do." Wollestone's eyes were very friendly, but there was a great uneasiness about them. "Shall we go into the chart-room, sir. Lot of noise here." He motioned the wind, the creaking cables and the clatter of a heavy pump forward, and led the way up a ladder to the bridge.

"Ah, that's better." Vane settled himself on a revolving stool and looked with love at the gleaming paint, the brass instruments, the atmosphere of unhurried efficiency. "Much better. Now, Paddy, how's it going?"

"Very well, sir, very well indeed. Under normal conditions and granting that the ship's papers are intact, there'd be not the slightest difficulty in getting them out. Only the first two compartments are flooded and the rest of the hull seems sound enough. They're pumping out the foul air now. As soon as the next shift takes over, they can start cutting through the bulkhead and begin looking for the safe. That is, if they do go down." He looked out to sea; the black cloud ridge was much higher now and seemed to be moving closer.

"May I ask Mr. Howard a question, sir? Thank you. Mr. Howard, I don't know if you are a sailor, but you must try and realise what the position now is. In about seven minutes, the present shift will come up, three men, and the next one will take over. They will work in the hull of that U-Boat for about half an hour. At any time during these thirty minutes the storm is liable to break. If it does, my duty will be quite clear. We are off a rocky and deeply shelving coast, at anchor. Those cables have about as much chance of holding, as a piece of string, if the storm hits us. My first consideration will be to save my ship. I will have to release the cables and put to sea, leaving those three divers to quite certain death. The chances of the storm striking during the next shift are about fifty, fifty. Mr. Howard, I have to know. Are those papers you want important enough to let me take that risk?"

Michael's mouth went very dry. He looked out at the sullen sea and the cloud bank behind it, and forced himself to speak.

"Yes, sir," he said, "yes, Captain Wollestone, I'm sorry but they are. I can't tell you why, I'm afraid. I'm under orders too, and in any case it's a long story, but I'm afraid you must take that risk."

"Very well, we are told to co-operate with you, the next shift will go down as scheduled." His eyes were suddenly very cold and hostile.

"Just a minute, Captain Wollestone. There's one more thing. Though I am unable to tell you the content of the papers we want, I think I can show you how much we do want them. I would like to have your permission to accompany the next party."

"What!" Wollestone wheeled incredulously at him. "No, a good gesture, but I'm afraid I cannot allow that."

"Just a minute, Paddy." Vane pulled himself heavily up from his stool and for a moment all traces of Lord Fisher had vanished.

"It is a very good gesture, you know, very good indeed." He crossed to Michael and tilted up his face. "Can see why he made it. If those men are left you'd feel like suicide, wouldn't you? Yes. Tell me, Howard, you're fit, are you? Heart, lungs all right?"

"Yes, sir, I think so."

"Very well. Come on, Paddy, let him go. I'll take the responsibility. Thought there was good stuff in him, Paddy. Grand nephew of old Hippo Howard, one of the best sea captains the service ever had, when you were footling around the Serpentine with your Nanny. All right, we'll get you fixed up, son. One more thing though—"

He stood back and looked very hard at Michael. "Not squeamish, are you? Not liable to vomiting. You know what you'll see when they get that bulkhead open, don't you?"

Once, years ago, Michael had spoken to a diver who had gone into the sunken hull of *Thetis* in Liverpool Bay. The description was very close to him now.

"No, sir," he said, "no, I'm not squeamish and I think I know what I'll see."

"Right, let's get cracking then. Take him down to the bosun, Paddy, and get him fixed up with his togs. Be seeing you, Howard."

The next five minutes were the shortest Michael had ever known in his life. He was hurried down on to the streaming deck, the pump panting and the cables creaking ominously now. And was introduced to a fatherly officer who helped him with the enormous weighted boots and the science fiction suit.

"It's quite easy, sir, nothing at all to worry about. All you've got to do is to follow George, Petty Officer Lord, sir." He indicated a diver standing poised at the edge of the deck, a wire above his head. "We're dead above the sub, sir, and it's all lit up down there, you'll see the air lock orl rite. Just go up the ladder into it and then George'll give you a hand off with your helmet. O.K., sir, well, good luck."

The helmet closed around him like a heavy football with the light dim through the glass panel in front of his eyes and an avid, invigorating tang of oxygen around him. Then the slings tightened on his shoulders, his leaden feet pulled away from him and he was riding up, moving out and dropping quickly down through dark water.

It was rather a pleasant sensation. The suit pressed tightly round him and there was no feeling of light, motion or sound. It was as if, in a second, all existence had ceased and death was just something dark, formless, yet conscious and secure. It wasn't for long. A little over a minute, perhaps, but it seemed like hours. Then the darkness ceased and there were lights on all sides of him. His feet hit bottom and he sank to his knees on a bed of very white sand, while his hands pressed against a rough red wall in front of him. For a moment he didn't know it was the submarine. There was something too natural about that huge mass, covered with shellfish and gleaming in damp rust, that made it look anything but man-made. Then he saw the conning tower in front of him and beyond it metal that was not rust. A bright steel vizor with a ladder reaching up to it.

He groped his way forward, half upright, half on his knees at times, with the cable dragging like a dead weight behind him and slowly pulled himself up the ladder; at each step into the air the weights on his legs seemed more unbearable. But at last he was there, there was a figure helping him, a wrench at his shoulders as the helmet was screwed off.

A homely face with blond hair was looking at him and there was a metallic snap as the harness came loose.

"You orl rite, sir. Just a tick while I get these off you." The man bent down and slipped the weights from Michael's feet. "That's better, ain't it. I think we best go into the 'ull now, sir. There's not room to think in 'ere, is there?"

Michael followed him through the ragged gash in the plate into a narrow tunnel packed tight with rusty cylinders, weed-covered machinery and bunks which had once been the crew's mess. There were dead fish on the deck and a crab scurried between his feet. From behind a cylinder, a bony arm, picked clean of flesh and clothing, stretched out to him.

The No. Three bulkhead was quite a long way into the ship where its lines broadened. Its door was welded solid with rust and in front of it he saw the blue stab of an acetylene flame as the two divers cut through the steel. They sang as they worked and rather incongruously he heard the tune of the "Mountains of Morne." There was a lot of cynicism in the words:

> "Oh, 'ere's to the lads on the mighty old Hood.
> That two funnel cruiser is no bloody good.
> I kissed me old mother and jined 'er today,
> But Greenland to London's an effing long way—"

They broke off as a bell whirred and a loudspeaker burst into life.

"This is the Captain speaking. Here are your final orders. When you have cut the bulkhead, go through into the main department and begin your search for the safe. It will most probably be in the chart locker, just aft and to port of the conning tower ladder. As soon as you have secured the safe to a line, you are to abandon the submarine and all the equipment you have down there, cutters, lights, everything, and return to *Hybrid*. Speed is essential, is that clear?"

The chief petty officer with the blond hair glanced at the cutting flame which was beginning to trace an amber line across the steel. He took up the microphone at his side.

"Your message clearly understood, sir. Cutting operations on the bulkhead are now in progress. I estimate the time of entry into main compartment as three minutes, sir." He replaced the phone and smiled at Michael.

"That means they're getting edgy up there, sir, don't want to pile the old *'Ibrid* up on that bloody cliff face. Must be breaking up there by now." He spat on the slime of the deck. "Cor, Gawd 'elp sailors on a night like this. You want to go in there with me, sir?" He glanced at the widening amber circle.

"Yes, I think so, Petty Officer Lord. Can't we send these two men up as soon as they've got through the door?"

"Well, I suppose so, but—" Lord looked doubtfully at Michael for a moment. "You know what you'll see in there, don't you, sir. Won't be nice."

"Yes, yes, I know what we'll see. Just give your order, please."

"Aye, aye, sir. As you say. You two, Willis and Bailey. Soon as you get an entrance for us, you can hook it. Just pass me a light when I get through and then beat it back to *'Ibrid*. Got that."

Without looking round they slowly nodded. The circle was nearly finished now.

The petty officer pulled a shielded light on a long run of flex forward and turned to the side.

"You'd best go first, sir," he said to Michael. "I'll look after the lamp, and see that these bleeders really do 'ook it.

"Ready, sir."

"Yes." Michael braced himself and watched the red line. It glowed white suddenly as the ends met and then as if on hinges the metal bent forward and fell with a clang.

As the two sailors stepped to the side, Michael sprang at the hole. Even through his thick gauntlets he could feel the hot bite of the metal as his hands clutched at the edge. Then he was through and standing in the darkness of the main hull.

It was the dryness that was different at first. Not slime, but firm, dry steel was under his feet. That and the air. Air hissing from the *Hybrid's* pumps, with a sweetish tang on it. He moved forward groping in the darkness and then stopped dead as the light went on.

"So this was it," he thought, "this was what it was really like." He shut his eyes for a moment and leaned heavily against a bulkhead. "It would be, of course, the lack of air would preserve them. But not like this. Oh God, he had never thought it would be like this. 'You are now in the bottom of the World,' said a voice from his own head. 'Right in the very bottom of the world. Wherever you go, you will never be deeper than this, because you are now standing in the very bottom of the world.' " He suddenly felt very cold and there was a grey taste in his mouth.

Long ago he had seen a picture about the loss of a submarine.

He remembered how, when all hope of rescue had been abandoned, the actors had died. They had resigned themselves to death, listened to a prayer reading by the captain and then quietly waited for the end. The camera had drawn away from those relaxed faces and the hull of the ship had become transparent giving a view of them calmly grouped together as the screen faded.

How false it had been; he had enjoyed it, then, been moved by it then, but now he would have liked to burn every inch of the film as he looked at the reality.

"You orl rite, sir." Lord hurried through the hole beside him. "Don't look at the pore blighters, sir. Just come in. Aft of the ladder, the Captain said it was. Let's get it." He dashed forward, pushing things out of his way as he went.

" 'Ere we are, sir. Got it, I think, yes, orl rite now, sir. This must be it. Hell, the bastards have fixed it to the bulkhead."

The safe was held tightly to the side by four large screws, it was obviously what they wanted and obviously quite immovable. On the wall above it there was a picture of a grey-haired woman and two small children. 'With my blessings to U.1760 and all who sail in her' was written underneath.

"Go back and get the cutter, sir. We'll have this lot orf in a tick." Lord started to fling equipment to the side to clear a space in front of the safe.

Michael pushed the cylinder through the opening and slid it along the deck, taking care the flame remained lit.

As he reached the safe, the loudspeaker behind them again burst into life. "Chief Petty Officer Lord, Forebridge here. Captain's orders to you and Mr. Howard. You are to abandon U-boat immediately, with or without safe. We are releasing cables in five minutes."

Lord turned up the flame and swung it on to the top left hand screw, he smiled as he watched it glow, run and begin to disintegrate. "That's one of them, sir." The flame shot down to the lower flange.

"Lord, why don't you answer." The voice on the speaker was hard with anxiety. "I repeat, you are to abandon U-boat immediately. Captain's orders."

"Shut up, you silly bleeder." Lord pushed in front of Michael and started work on the other side of the safe. "Three. Soon as this one goes, sir, you take that end and we 'op it quick. Right, come on." The last screw gave and the box clattered heavily on to the deck. Michael seized the end and together they half carried, half dragged it forward. Lifting it with care through the hole in the bulkhead and then on towards the air lock, with their feet slipping and stumbling on the greasy metal. The loudspeaker still blared orders as they passed it and then suddenly the tone of the voice changed. "Goodbye, now, God bless you both," it said.

But at last they were there. Lord tied the safe carefully to a line and threw it down through the air lock. He grinned as he watched it sink and then begin to drag upwards.

"Right you are, sir, mission completed, now we 'ook it. Never bother about these. He kicked aside the weights and picked up one of the helmets. "We got no time for them now. Just 'ang on to the 'arness, 'old yer breath and pray as you've never ruddy prayed before. All right, you above, pull us in now." He shouted into the microphone in his helmet. Then he pointed down, grasped his end of the harness and together they leapt for the hole as the ropes jerked in their hands.

They only just made it. The line ran forward like a whip lash, dragging them hard against the lip of the air lock, and for a moment Michael felt his grip giving. Then he was clear. Rising as in a lift through the dark water with a terrible pain in his chest, till at last the darkness broke into grey, pounding waves, and he felt fresh air on his face and fell heavily on to something hard and unyielding. He opened his eyes and looked up from *Hybrid's* deck, as with slipped cables she tore out to sea. The first thing he saw was Lord's grinning face beside him. Then another face, dark and scowling came between them.

"Well, you've certainly taken your bloody time about it, young man," said Admiral Vane.

CHAPTER ELEVEN

"Therefore, upon receipt of the instructions from Grand Admiral Karl Doenitz, you are hereby requested and required to carry out this assignment with all due expedition."

Although the German navy was of recent growth and tradition, the wording of its official documents was as archaic as that of the British. Kirk scowled at the sprawling signature at the foot of the sheet and then pushed it back into its folder.

"Well, ladies and gentlemen," he said. "That is almost the end of the story. Now, let's have a look at the beginning, as far as we know it, of course." He glanced up at the four people in the room.

In the corner, by the window, were Michael and Dr. Reade, while Vickers, the Minister's secretary, leaned gracefully against the mantelpiece. Beside Kirk's desk, feet out, sprawling in the only comfortable chair in the room, was Admiral Vane.

"I've asked you here, because as you are all officially involved in this business, I think it only fair that you should know what seems to have gone before. You, doctor, because you are the representative from the hospital where at least three of these cases have originated. You, Mr. Vickers as the representative of the Ministry. You, Admiral Vane." He permitted himself a slight grin. "Because of the friendly cooperation which you have given to this department.

"Now, what present figure have you got, Mike?"

"Seventeen, sir. There was another chap in Liverpool this morning."

"Thank you. That is seventeen murders in the last two weeks. Murders with no rational explanation and which were always followed by the suicide or death of the killer. Manic killings, as far as we can see, because there always appeared to be some form of mental instability in the killer, and something about the victim which aggravated this instability. That is the surface motive for these acts, but it tells us nothing, nothing at all. As far as we are concerned, they are still murders without rhyme—ladies and gentlemen—or reason. It is up to use to find the reason. The why, where and how of it all."

He paused for a moment and leaned back in his chair, looking hard at their faces.

"Yes, the why, where and how. The second of these is easy. It all started here in this office, when the first victim rang me up and promised me a certain piece of information. I didn't get it, so we'll leave it for a moment and go back to the original point, why. Tell me Mr. Reade. Does the name Erich Rhine mean anything to you?"

"Rhine, Erich Rhine. Let me think for a moment." A slight furrow spread across her face.

"Yes, it conveys a little, not much, but I seem to remember reading a treatise by somebody of that name. There was very little known about him, I think. Was he perhaps a zoologist? Yes, I did read his treatise, but it was a long time ago. He had been studying the methods of migration and communication between animals. Extra sensory perception, that kind of thing. There was quite a lot about telepathic waves between groups of insects. It was all very interesting but I don't think it would hold water. No, I don't think his conclusions were valid. Is that the man you mean, General?"

"Yes, Doctor, that is probably the man, and he may also be our beginning, the key to the why. Let's see what we can piece together, so far.

"Early in nineteen forty-four, our opponents across the North Sea struck on a very jolly idea. They felt that it would be an excellent thing if certain undesirable persons, such as the Allied leaders, were removed by assassination. At first they considered using hired killers for this purpose, but because the risk was too great, it proved impossible. Therefore they looked for another way, not hired killers, but true, dedicated fanatics. After a time they found them. To be brief, they intended to use psychopaths.

"Yes, not a very pleasant thought, is it?" He paused as Vane blew his nose violently.

"For this purpose, a number of patients from various asylums were selected and a research station was formed for their training—I use that word for want of a better. It was near Herford, and the officer in charge was not a psychologist in the proper sense of the word. It was our friend, Erich Rhine, the zoologist, about whom we know so little, apart from his interest in extra sensory perception."

"But why, General Kirk? I don't see what he, what Rhine could achieve." Reade's face was alive with concentration.

"No, Doctor, none of us do yet; shall we go on?

"At about the time this place at Herford was opened, there was a British traitor, named John Glyde, engaged in propaganda broadcasts from Radio Hamburg. He also did a great deal of work in P.O.W. camps. Yes, Admiral, as you say, the bastard.

"We know quite a lot about Glyde, now. He was a bad man, probably the one really evil man who has come my way, but he had a certain very interesting quality. Everybody who knew him tells us the same thing. When you were with Glyde he seemed able to exert a form of influence over you which made his thoughts, his wishes, at times, seem the most important thing in the world. It could almost be described as a kind of impersonal hypnosis. That is why he was so very useful to them in the camps.

"During the summer of forty-four, Glyde seemed to suffer a mental and physical decline. He was removed from his duties at Hamburg, and two weeks later his colleagues were informed that he was dead. That was incorrect. He was taken to a nursing home near Munich and kept there under observation. Later he was transferred to this place at Herford.

"Well, we don't know what happened to him there. The building was bombed by the R.A.F. and all the records vanished. All we know is this. While he was there something was done to Glyde. Something that altered him. A treatment that altered him completely."

"What do you mean? What treatment?" Reade stared at him. "What was done? You know, I think I may be getting warmer now. Rhine was the man in charge, wasn't he? The extra sensory business. Glyde had some kind of telepathic power and they tried to increase it, to use it on their—their experimental subjects, was that it?"

"Possibly, Doctor, but we can't be sure yet. We know nothing yet. We merely marshal our few facts and hope they will fit together." Kirk glanced at his notes for a moment.

"Let's go on. Somehow, Glyde survived the bombing, and after that was kept hidden away under conditions of the utmost secrecy till almost the end of the war. He was looked after by a kind of half guard, half attendant called Paul Vanek. Yes, Doctor, that was the brother of your Vanek, who went to Berlin three weeks ago and spoke to him. He asked him to identify a certain mark on Glyde's hand, a scar like a stigmata which he had got in a café brawl. When he had the information he wanted he returned to England to tell me about it. As you all know, he never reached me, but we were able to trace his steps. I sent Mr. Howard to Berlin and he spoke to Paul Vanek. He got a few facts from him; not many because the man was drunk and before he could finish talking somebody put a knife through his chest. His last words were rather significant, though, as they seemed to suggest that right at the end of the war, Glyde, or what he had become, was taken out of Germany on a U-boat."

"A U-boat, General." Vane seemed to wake up with a snort. "You mean that was the joker we cut up for you."

"That's right, Admiral Vane, the U1760, which you were good enough to cut up for us. It appears that her regular commander was a certain Leutnant Gortz, but we needn't concern ourselves about him. As I have told you, he was relieved of his command a few hours before she put to sea, and handed over to Capitan zur See, Phillip von Euhlenburg. A most gallant officer this man Euhlenburg seems to have been. Good record. Iron Cross, forty-two. Knight's Cross with oak leaves the following year. Yes, for that last voyage they wanted somebody who would carry out instructions to the letter, who would fight to the very end and not count the cost."

He rummaged in the folder and brought out a single sheet of notepaper. It was covered in neat, though somewhat cramped handwriting in green ink.

"This is the most important document we have got so far. If we do beat this thing it will probably be due to this one slip of paper. I would like you, Admiral, to convey my thanks to everybody on *Hybrid* who helped to get it for us. Now I will read it to you. It bears the address Flensburg and is undated. Please forgive my quick translation."

"Dear von Euhlenburg,

"By now you will have reached Bergen and taken over the command of the U1760. I was personally more than sorry to have had to ask the Grand Admiral to give you this order, but it is imperative that the ship is commanded by an officer in whom we have utter confidence.

"As it is now likely that the Führer has died fighting with his troops in Berlin, it is up to us who remain to make a final effort to bring pressures on our enemies which may compel them to grant a just and honourable peace to our unhappy fatherland.

"Your mission, my dear von Euhlenburg, concerns such a pressure, though I fear I cannot give you any further details. Here are your instructions.

"As soon as the plane carrying the cargo and our agent who will be known to you as No. 666 reaches Bergen, you will take them aboard and proceed at once to point on the coast of Scotland called Spey Inlet at Position four, seven eight degrees West, eight, eight, two degrees North. Charts and the latest Intelligence Reports as to minefields are attached.

"Having reached this position, you will lie submerged till six a.m. Greenwich Mean Time on May 3rd, when you will surface and convey our agent and the cargo ashore. At the far side of the cliff, marked with an X on the chart, you will find a road. At exactly 6.30, a van will be waiting at a point on the road nearest to the sea. You will approach the driver of the van and ask him if he is Mr. James O'Sullivan. If the answer is in the affirmative, you will hand over the cargo and No. 666 to him and return to the U-boat.

"Once your mission is completed you are at liberty to take your command to any port which we still control. It is essential, however, that throughout the operation, your officers and crew are not informed of the cargo they are carrying.

"Believe me, my dear Euhlenburg, I much regret giving you an order which may very likely cost you your life, but I

am assured of its necessity both for the Party and the Fatherland. Adieu."

Very carefully, Kirk tucked the paper back into its folder.

"Once again, please excuse my translation. Apart from its content, there are two things which are significant about this document. The signature is that of Heinrich Himmler, and as you will
remember: three sixes is the mark of the Beast."

For a moment there was silence in the room, and then came
the voice of loud, arrogant, down to earth reality.

"A cargo the chaps weren't to be told about, eh. Sounds cheerful." Vane glowered from his chair, his eyebrows working. "Well,
sir, what was the cargo? Some sort of bomb, destructive apparatus, that it? Kind of secret weapon."

"In a sense, Admiral, in a sense a secret weapon, but not quite
what you mean. Not a piece of apparatus. I think they landed
Glyde. John Glyde, or the thing he had become."

"The thing he had become. Do you mind explaining yourself,
General Kirk? I must say I'm still completely at sea." Vane started
to rise from his chair and then sat back at a look from Kirk.

"No, I cannot explain. I know no more than you do. That's
why I have asked somebody to help us. I've given him all the facts
we've got and he should be ready now. I am hoping he may be
able to provide the 'how.' " Kirk walked across the office and
opened the door to his private room which lay behind.

"If you are finished, perhaps you would come through now,
Professor."

Although Michael had been with Professor Claude Ranier for
at least an hour that morning, he still felt mirth rising as he looked
at him, for the man was half dressed.

Above decks all was well. The mass of iron grey hair was a
trifle long, but neatly combed. The heavy intellectual face was
shaven and the spectacles were steel rimmed and unostentatious.
Below the face he wore a stiff white collar, a dark speckled tie and
a double-breasted coat with a carnation buttonhole. Cut off from
the waist he could have been a city business man on his way to the
office. But the waist was the end of the Professor's compromise
to society. Below the edge of the coat there was a thin ridge of

short, very short khaki trunks, running into an expanse of hairy, rather bow legs, which terminated in green golf socks and heavy brogues. He was like the finished product in a child's game of Heads and Bodies. He seemed quite oblivious of the effect of his appearance, however, beaming at the company and bowing deeply as Kirk made the introductions.

"Well, I don't think I need tell anyone why I asked Professor Ranier to help us. I'm sure you all know of him by reputation." Kirk had the manner of a headmaster introducing the governors to the assembled school.

"Of course." Vickers smiled complacently from the mantelpiece, and Dr. Reade's face was full of devotion.

"Right, now Professor, you've been through the facts as far as we know them. Would you be kind enough to let us have your comments?"

"Just a minute, General Kirk. 'Fraid I'm out of all this." Vane sat bolt upright in his chair, goggling at Ranier's legs. With great difficulty he forced his eyes upwards.

"Sorry, but I don't know who you are. Let me see. Professor Ranier?" He gave the name its full English pronunciation. "Yes, seen a picture of your—your face somewhere. Heard the name vaguely. Rings a faint bell, but I can't say I know anything about you. Perhaps you'd be kind enough to tell me."

For a full minute Ranier appeared deaf. He took off his glasses and polished them with a large, mauve handkerchief. Then he replaced them with care and looked long and hard at Vane. He might have been inspecting an interesting laboratory specimen.

"So, you do not know who I am M'sieu l'Admiral. How shall I put it. Yes, I am the man who knows, the expert."

For a moment Vane seemed in danger of a stroke. His face took on a blackish tinge and a strangling sound came from his throat. Kirk hastened to pass over the incident.

"Perhaps I'd better explain. Professor Ranier is the Head of the Institut Nationale in Paris dealing with Mental Diseases. He is also the author of a number of standard works on extra-physical phenomena. He is the expert in the sense that he is the world's greatest authority on that subject."

"Thank you, and now after that interruption, shall we continue with the business in hand?" Ranier flicked a sheaf of papers from his pocket and squinted at them. "When you first tele-phoned me about this business, General, I was frankly sceptical. I came, because it is after all my subject, and I always enjoy a trip to London at the expense of your Government. Now I am almost sure that you may have just hit on something which I have sus-pected for a great many years." He took a short blackened pipe from his pocket and lit it with care. Harsh, choking smoke rose to the ceiling as he went on.

"Yes, I have almost thought it might be possible to find the area. Now it seems that somebody has beaten me to it."

"The area? Professor, could you be a little more explicit?"

"Sorry, I was, as you say, talking to myself. The area of of the brain that controls these things. These things which are known to exist but are still not understood at all. Telepathy in fact, General. A communication which requires no physical transmitter, but which can be as clear as day. There are too many cases to doubt its existence, but nothing to show how it works."

He pulled himself up on to the table and sat down on it, his bare legs dangling incongruously from the edge, but there was suddenly nothing amusing about him.

"Today, gentlemen, we are inclined to laugh at the beliefs of primitive peoples. We talk about savages and mumbo jumbo, and the dark ages. We sometimes think that the ancient Greeks were the only race who did any serious thinking because they were free from superstition. In nearly every case we would be right. I repeat that. In nearly every case. Let us dismiss ninety-nine point nine per cent of the medieval sorcerers, the negro witch doctors, the fakirs as imposters, and there is still that little point nought, nought one per cent that makes us wonder; that we cannot dismiss. If we find that that single instance is proven, then——"

"Then, Professor." Dr. Reade craned forward expectantly.

"Then, my dear, it all becomes true. The negro witch doctor can harm his victim without physical contact across a hundred miles of land. The witch's doll is not a fairy tale but a very real force. The man does wither with a curse as the ship nears land.

"Yes, it may exist, this force. This communication without

physical contact, without the senses being involved, and more than that—" His pipe rapped suddenly on the desk.

"Much more. If all that is granted. Possession. Possession of the soul, the personality, the unconscious becomes quite credible."

"But how, Professor? In our present case, how does this fit? Glyde, the killings, this man Rhine?" Kirk looked up from his note taking.

"I don't know, General. I don't know at all, I merely guess. I am quite an old man now and I have been studying these matters for most of my life. But I still know nothing. You see, there is one basic difficulty. This thing follows no known laws and unlike other forms of communication, such as speech or radio, it appears to have no physical transmitter. Because of this, we are still in the dark as to its origin. We have tried to explain it in a number of ways. Some form of time-space sequence for example, but we have never really succeeded. I wonder if Rhine used a much simpler way and found the answer."

"But how, Professor? What could he have done?"

"I don't know that, Doctor, but I will risk a guess. Perhaps by simple surgery. Perhaps he found an area of the brain that controls these things and used it. After all, why not? Why should such a place not exist? It does for everything else, doesn't it? Smell, sight, even conscience. If it exists, and if he found it, then it would be easy. He would enlarge it. He would use injections perhaps, or radiation, it depends. It is a thousand to one that he would kill his subject, but if not, if he lived and was a man like this man, Glyde, whom you have described to me, a potential telepath already, a carrier of this force, then ça va. Then you might get a situation almost exactly the same as you have shown to me, General Kirk."

"Thank you. Thank you very much, Professor Ranier. There are two points I would like to know. Firstly, can this communication work both ways? You see, our—our enemy has always been one jump ahead of us. Vanek comes to talk to me and he is killed. His brother in Berlin begins to speak to Mr. Howard and he also dies. All the time it seemed as if our actions were being watched in advance."

"And why not, General? Granted one thing, the other is

simple. Thought reading would go with it. It always has done. Why, there are adepts among the Australian tribes who pride themselves on the power to read a man's mind over five hundred miles of space."

"And your second point."

"The time lag, Professor. It is fourteen years since Glyde was heard of. If what you say is correct, if Glyde became this carrier, then why didn't something happen before?"

"How do we know? How can we know what the processes were? He was altered wasn't he? Whatever was done to him, left him paralysed, physically and mentally. Perhaps the shock was too much, but after fourteen years he might have recovered and found his power. Once that had happened, I don't think it would take him long to use it."

"And the fact that it is the mentally unbalanced who are affected, Professor?" Reade leaned forward in her chair.

"My dear Doctor, you are supposed to be a psychiatrist." He looked at her with disapproval. "Surely it is obvious. As you must know in certain forms of mental illness there is a kind of vacuum in the brain which is very liable to suggestion. How easy for this thing to creep into that vacuum and possess it. Remember besides what kind of a man Glyde was. General Kirk has described him as truly evil. Remember also what had been done to him. He had been subjected to some form of treatment that had almost destroyed him both physically and mentally. I think that when he recovered, he might feel a kinship towards insanity. A desire to take over the fears and hatreds of other crippled minds and merge them with his own. It might also be a practice ground, a form of sport."

"A form of sport?"

"Yes, just that. He needs practice and he needs relaxation. Half these cases have been purely illogical and wanton, it seems. The others very clever and well thought out. We have two sides of a personality to deal with, I think. One is that of a deranged child, and the other is possibly that of a genius."

"Thank you. That is what I wanted to know." Kirk turned to the window and looked down on the crawling traffic. "How are we to stop this, Professor Ranier?"

"That is your job. There is only one way. By finding this thing that was once Glyde. Finding it and destroying it utterly. And moreover, General, finding it quickly." He glanced at his notes, and then stuffed them back into his pocket.

"At every minute we waste talking here, this thing is gaining strength. Your cases increase. At first they were in one area, now they begin to spread. And more than spread. At the moment they only appear to affect a small group of the community, the mentally diseased, but very soon that may alter." He looked hard at all of them and he was no longer a slightly comic figure, but tremendously impressive.

"Soon that may alter and then it will be no longer just a small section of the community that is affected. If that happens I am afraid you will have something on your hands that will make the Black Death look like a mild epidemic of influenza."

"Don't worry." Kirk swung round from the window. "We'll find it."

"Oh yes, you'll find it. I'm quite certain of that. You'll find it, given time." Ranier knocked his pipe out on the ashtray. "The only thing is, mon General, I don't think anybody is going to give you any time at all."

At six a.m. on the following morning, a man called Roberts woke up and looked at his wife asleep beside him. They had been married for more years than either of them cared to remember and every line of her face, every turn of the expression was familiar to him. Yet that morning it was different, quite different. It was as if there was a complete stranger lying beside him.

He got out of bed and very gently pulled back the curtains so as not to wake her and then leaned over.

For a long time he watched the sleeping face, and then suddenly he knew. He knew with utter certainty who she was and what he had been fooled and deceived by all these years. He reeled for a moment against the bedside table with the horror of what he saw.

The woman wakened with the noise and looked at him.

"Good morning, dear," she said, "you're awake very early." She glanced at the clock and then suddenly stared at him.

"Peter," she said. "What are you doing? No, Peter, you're hurting. Please, Peter, my throat, oh Peter—"

They were both dead by the time the clock struck seven.

CHAPTER TWELVE

As the newsagent had promised, the copies of the Tynecastle papers arrived with the morning post. Penny threw them on the table and reluctantly prepared to read them during breakfast. By now the charm of the idea had worn off and seemed no more than a bit of nonsense brought on by a sleepless night.

Still, there could be something in it. It was odd, so many of the killings taking place in that one small area. Michael had told her that the 'thing' whatever it was would not be influenced by space, so it was very odd. There might be some slight, unobserved piece of information tucked away behind the headlines of the local news which would prove a clue. Also she'd paid for the damned things, so she might as well get her money's worth. She slipped the jam knife through the wrappers and started to read.

There were only two papers, the *Tyneside Observer* and the *Evening Record*. Both their front pages were covered with details of the killings and she went through them with care. Nothing new. They had obviously been asked by the police to use a soft pedal. There was nothing that was not reported more fully and accurately by the London Press. She turned over the pages to the dreary items of local news.

The editors of the *Observer* and the *Record* obviously worked closely together. Each spot of local interest was faithfully recorded by both papers though with widely different styles.

Like its famous namesake, the *Observer* was sober, quietly spoken and refined. Not so the *Record*, which smacked of what used to be known as the gutter press. Between them they gave the dreary flashes of civic chambers, police courts and sport an air of unreality.

"Scavenger on assault charge," stated the *Observer* chastely. "Dustman was Human Beast," shouted the *Record*. "Incumbent mentioned in Will," said the *Observer*, "Windfall for Priest," chirruped the *Record*.

Penny flicked through them and there was nothing at all. She didn't really know what she was looking for. Some slight reference, perhaps some passing mention of a name, a face, which might give her a lead, but there was nothing, nothing that helped. Still, she kept on at it, reading each paragraph with care and boredom. At the last page of the *Observer*, tucked away beneath the opening of a new sewage disposal plant, there was a thin headline. 'Final Reading at the West Gatesend Literary Society'. With the air of completing a dull task faithfully she read on down the column.

"Yesterday's meeting of the Society began with a reading of the concluding chapters of Mr. Allan Cawdor's novel, 'Untimely Ripped', which we understand is to be published by Messrs. Malcolm and Donaldbain during the coming spring. Mr. Cawdor's style is strong if somewhat sad and Mrs. Brocker, the president, predicted that the book would prove an immediate success."

"Good for you, Cawdor old boy," said Penny and wearily read on. 'Blar, blar, blar.'

"Miss Shirley Newton delighted the audience with the reading of her short story, 'Playing with Fire'. This tells of the experience of a spiritualist medium who becomes possessed by her spirit control; only at the end of this beautifully written piece, does Madame Agatha, the medium, realise what is happening to her, when in a nightmare she seems to see the image of the control. He is described as a young man with a beautiful but evil face, bearing on his hand the mark of a stigmata.

"Miss Newton was warmly congratulated by members of the group for this exciting and original piece of work. She said it had come to her on the spur of the moment and had very nearly written itself.

"Mr. Coate's rather long humourless poem, 'Flung in a heap by a far-flung Geisha' followed next, it is—"

Penny switched back to the account of the story and read it through again.

"It couldn't be that. It must be mere coincidence. The stigmata. It was just the kind of symbol which would be used by a neurotic exhibitionist who wrote stories for a literary group. Still that scar she had seen in Vanek's photograph, it had looked just

like that. The nail, the ice pick, the same wound. That and possession, possession by a young man with a beautiful but evil face."
She threw down the paper and opening a drawer pulled out an
envelope of family photographs.

"No, you couldn't say beautiful. John wasn't beautiful. It was
a neat, self contained, compact face, with something wrong with
it. Evil perhaps, but only because she knew his story. Still, given a
big dose of Miss Newton's poetical imagination."

She got up from the table, lit a cigarette and tried to think.

"And possession, that was how Michael had described it to her
after the meeting with that French professor. It was a hundred to
one chance of there being any connection, no, a thousand to one.
But at this stage, with the death roll increasing every day, every
chance was worth trying."

She picked up the phone and dialled a number.

As always she got through much quicker than any normal call
and as always there was the same completely anonymous voice
answering her. A voice from which it was impossible to tell the
age, personality or even sex of its owner.

"Hullo," said the voice. "This is extension five nine. What can
we do for you? Oh, Mr. Howard, no, I'm afraid he is not available
at the moment. Is there anybody else who could help, or could I
take a message?"

"Could I speak to"—Penny started to ask for Kirk and then
broke off. It was ridiculous. She couldn't bother Kirk on a hunch
like this. Besides, even supposing it was true, did she want him?
Did she want either him or Michael? This was her business, now.
Her own business. As if obeying an order her hand moved forward and dropped the phone back on its rest.

She picked up the paper again and looked at the last paragraph.
"The next meeting of the Society will take place on Saturday, the
twelfth, at the Stone House Café in Redfern Row at six-thirty."
Saturday the twelfth, that was today. They kept themselves pretty
busy in West Gatesend Literary circles. Six-thirty. Only just after
ten now, that gave her plenty of time and the Riley had been
tuned last week. She hurried out of the flat and across the yard to
where Tony Field was bending over a decrepit Morris saloon. He
straightened and grinned as she came to him.

"Lo, partner. Got those wretched tax accounts fixed yet?
I hope to hear we've been losing money like water lately."

"No, not yet, they'll have to wait a day or two. Look, Tony. I'm running out on you again, just for a night. You'll manage O.K., won't you?"

"Sure, I'll manage. Real little gadabout, aren't you, since the new boy friend took over. Where to this time? Not Berlin again?"

"No, not Berlin. Just Gatesend."

"Gatesend. Cor, can't he do better than that? I can think of a lot of places to take a girl, and not one of them's called Gatesend."

"Shut up, Tony, it's not like that, purely business and I'm going alone. Be an angel and fill the Riley up for me, will you?"

"Enchanté, Madame." He bowed deeply, clicked his heels and wiped his greasy hands on his overalls. "Business, eh. If you see a nice Daimler hearse up there, going cheap, grab it, will you?"

"Sure, Tony, thanks a lot." She turned and ran back into the flat.

She changed quickly into her best black costume. Something rather severe and business-like, but still prosperous was wanted, she felt; then throwing a sponge bag and a nightdress into a case she was ready except for one thing, the one professional touch which would make all the difference. She picked up the telephone again.

"Hullo, get me the newsdesk, will you. Thanks. Newsdesk, could I speak to Miss Murdock, please. Mrs. Wise. Thanks, I'll hold on."

For perhaps two minutes she waited and then at last Poppy Murdock's hoarse, gin-ruined voice rattled across the wires.

"Yes, yes. Oh, it's you, Penny, how are you, sweetie! Such ages since we met, do let's try and fix something soon. I've got oodles of scandal to tell you. Honestly, just oodles. Did you hear about poor old Cynthia? No really, well listen."

Penny listened patiently as the stream of Half Truth, Untruth and rank, obscene libel was poured out over most of their mutual friends and acquaintances. At last she could bear it no longer and cut rudely into the middle of a disgusting and hair-raising account of what had happened to the wife of a perfectly respectable Member of Parliament.

"Look, Poppy, sorry to interrupt, but I've heard that one. What I wanted to ask you is if you could do me a favour?"

"A favour, but darling, of course, anything." The voice dropped half a tone. "But of course you do realise how ruddy badly we're paid in this beastly racket, don't you?"

"Don't be a B.F. Poppy, it's not money. I could probably buy you up any day of the week," said Penny somewhat tactlessly. "No, the fact is that I want to borrow your Press card."

"My pass, but Sweetie, what on earth for? It's no good for any shows, you know, worse luck. What can you want with it?"

Penny wracked her brains and gave Miss Murdock a fictitious account of the doings of an ex-boy friend who was appearing at the Law Courts and whose fall she dearly wished to witness.

The revenge aspect worked like a charm.

"But of course, Penny, I quite understand. I'd like to see the devil get his deserts myself, but I'm all tied up this afternoon, worse luck. Tell you what, meet me in the Wheatsheaf saloon in say half an hour, and we'll have a drink and a sandwich and I'll hand over. All right, goodbye, darling."

"Goodbye, sweetest." Penny replaced the phone with distaste and grabbing her bag, hurried down to the waiting car.

It was already late when she finally turned the Riley out of the wilderness of North London into the main road. Poppy Murdock had wanted her pound of flesh for the card in the shape of many martinis, club sandwiches and interminable conversation. The dashboard clock showed twelve-thirty as the last stretch of ribbon development fell back and she was able to press the accelerator down to the floorboard.

"Still, not too bad," she thought. Whatever his faults, Tony Field was a fine mechanic and the car had never gone better. Two hundred miles. Say a nice easy average of fifty. Get there about fiveish. Time to find a decent hotel, clean up and present herself as a seeker of culture by a quarter past six. It was all probably a bit of nonsense, a wild goose chase, a waste of time. But if not, if it wasn't nonsense, if she was really on to something, then—

She smiled slightly to herself and leaned back in her seat oblivious to everything except the traffic, the whine of the tyres, and her own thoughts, as the beautifully smooth twin camshaft engine hurled her north.

CHAPTER THIRTEEN

"Of course, Minister. Yes, I quite understand your feelings, and I agree with them. It has been a slow business. Fifteen years too slow, in fact, but I think we're almost home now. We've got all we need at last, and it's just a question of fitting the bits together.

"Yes, of course I'll ring you just as soon as there is something definite. Given a little luck it might be in the morning. Very well. Goodnight, Minister."

Kirk dropped the phone back on to its rest as if he were handling a rather disgusting object and sat down again.

"Little Boy Blue, come blow your horn, the sheep's in the meadow, the cow's in the corn," he said softly.

"And where is the man who looks after the sheep? He's down in the meadow fast asleep." His hand drummed slowly on the desk and he smiled at Michael. "Oh no, he's not, Mike. Not any longer. The man's wide awake at last and very soon he's going to pull Little Boy Blue in."

Since they had talked to Ranier, the change in both Kirk and Michael was extraordinary. The news couldn't have been worse. Eight more outbreaks had been reported that morning, and at last the public was beginning to grow restless. There had been stones thrown through the windows of a London police station, and a near riot in a Northern town. Yet, for all that they looked confident and untroubled because at last they knew exactly what they were up against. The period of groping in the dark was over at last and they were two professionals dealing with something they understood perfectly.

Michael stood by the map on the wall and stared at the tip of Scotland.

"Well, sir, I think we can assume that the U1760 did complete its mission and he was dropped here on the morning of May 22nd. The question now is, how did they get him out of the area?"

"Just a minute, Mike, just a minute. Give me time to think." Kirk pulled hard at his cigar. His rather washed out, pale blue eyes were very keen and hard. When he spoke his words seemed far away and quite divorced from the matter in hand.

"You know, Mike," he said. "When I was a kid, I had a hobby. I used to collect Eastern weapons. You know the kind of thing, Chinese daggers with corkscrew blades and lion-headed handles. Swords which were so heavy that it was all you could do to lift the bloody things, let alone do anyone in with 'em. Well, this business reminds me of those weapons in a way. You see, half their threat is fear. Fear not of the injury they can cause, but of themselves. Fear of the Lion, the devil-mask on the handle. Fear of the unknown. And we've been like that. We've been pottering round trying to imagine what was causing this thing, and we've been wasting our energies on just that. Now we can stop wondering and get to work, because we know. We know what the force is, and we also know that it has a cause, a carrier if you like, that exists in time and space. So let's get on and find it."

He pulled himself up from his chair and walked to the map. He looked at the inlet of water where the submarine had surfaced and taking a pencil from his pocket drew a heavy black circle around it.

"Right, that's where we start. Now let's see the difficulties which this chap Mr. James O'Sullivan would have had to get his cargo out of the area. You've been on to the War Office, haven't you? What was the position?"

"It would have been very difficult, sir." Michael glanced at his notebook and then looked back at the map.

"The whole area was still a restricted zone at the time, needing a special pass to enter or leave it. If we are to suppose that he picked up, whatever it was, on this side-road to the Cape Wrath lighthouse, there are only two alternative routes he could have taken. He could have headed south towards Lairg or Scourie or North to Thurso, but in each case he would have met a road block. Here at a place called Archreisgill, and here at Heilim." He drew two crosses on the map.

"I see. That means that it was virtually impossible for our friend to leave the area by car. Quite impossible, unless he was a person with a pass. A bona fide and regular entrant into the area. Yes, that should narrow our field down a little, I think. Now let's think who he could have been. A local tradesman, perhaps, taking supplies out to the lighthouse and the outlying farms."

"Sorry, sir." Michael shook his head. "I'm afraid that's out. There was a delivery van to the farms, but it didn't go out that day. Only on Mondays and Fridays. At the time in question it was in a garage with a broken spring. I checked with the local police. I know it's a long time ago, but they were quite definite about it. The lighthouse supplies were sent up every fortnight by a Trinity House lorry from Ullapool."

"Um. Very helpful of our friends the police to be so definite after thirteen years. Still, I suppose we must accept their word for it. Now, how else could it have been done? A farmer with a van, perhaps. No, it won't do. I know that country, they don't run to motor vehicles on the whole, and besides everybody knows everybody else. No German agent could go barging in and say he was old Fergus MacFerguson from Scourie. It must have been done from outside. Someone with a pass from outside."

He moved to the window and looked out. His cigar a faint glowing point in the dusk among the millions of other points which were springing up as the town prepared for night.

"Let's look at it from their point of view, Mike. How would we do it, if we had been in their shoes. Remember how we got Kretchmer out of Budapest. No, damn it, that don't work. Our scheme entailed a big land frontier and ample preparation. This was done in a small area and the time they had to prepare for it was infinitesimal. Remember Himmler's letter. The U-boat commander was told that only Hitler's death set the plan into operation. All the same, there's got to be a way through. Let's imagine that their agent gets his orders about two days before the meeting with the submarine. He is instructed to get a conveyance and pick up his cargo in a restricted zone in the north-westerly tip of Scotland. That means he is someone of some importance and position over here." His hand beat three times against the window frame. "And I thought I got the lot of them."

"Just a minute, sir, listen. I think I've got it." Michael moved quickly to him and stood by the window as in the distance there came the quick clanging of a bell. They leaned out over White-hall as it grew in volume and then faded as the flashing light of the ambulance shot past them and disappeared into the square.

"Yes, perhaps you have. Good boy." Kirk pulled down the window with a bang and stumped back to his desk. "Very good. Why the hell didn't I think of it before. Easy as falling off a log. No difficulty at all. Get a van, rig it up as an ambulance. Drive like hell with a lot of flashing lights and bells and no damn picket is likely to interfere with you. Particularly if on the return journey you happen to have a bona fide invalid in the back. And why a van, Mike? Why not a proper honest to God pukka ambulance, complete with yourself, a qualified and well documented doctor in the cab? Why not? A most sane and proper method of attack, does our friend credit." He picked up the house telephone and scowled at it.

"I just want two more little details and I think we should be ready to move in. Hullo, just hold on the line for a moment, Florrie. While I'm busy here, Mike, get through to that Inspector Jackson at Tynecastle, he's the only intelligent one in the station. Tell him I'll speak to him in a minute." He turned his attention to the phone in his hand.

"Now, Florrie, my dear. I've got some deadly dull work for you, but it may turn out to be the most important thing you'll ever do in your life, so be on your toes, girl. Right, go down to the records department and dig me out a list of all members of the medical profession who were even remotely suspected of Nazi leanings in any form. No, no, not the Brixton boys, just the people we weren't able to pull in for lack of proof. Good; and Florrie, by medical profession I don't mean just doctors, but nurses, orderlies, bone setters, in fact Uncle Tom Cobley and all. Yes, quick as you can, dear."

He dropped the receiver into its rest as Michael laid the outside line in front of him.

"They're just getting Jackson, sir. Take about five minutes they said. Tell me, what are you on to?"

"I don't know, boy. I think I've got something, but before I'm sure enough to take action, I must have two things quite straight. Think of Vanek a moment. The first Vanek who phoned us. We knew he would be on the Harwich train because he told us so. But how did anybody else know? If Jackson can assure us on that point and if Florrie digs up something of interest, then we may say 'from a view to a death in the morning'."

At the end of the wire a tiny voice began to murmur metallically as Kirk reached for it. "Hullo, Inspector. Sorry to dig you out, but I want a bit of co-operation. I think we're almost at the end of the line. What I want is this. The post office which deals with the hospital mail. What is it like? I see, small effort, part sweet shop, part tobacconist, only two assistants. Yes, I know the kind of place and thank God for it. Now listen. I want you to get round to that post office now. Talk to the assistants and try and find out if any telegram from either Germany or Holland was delivered to the hospital between the dates of September second and fourth. Good God, man, I don't care if they are shut up. Get to them. Dig the blighters out of bed if needs be; from what I've been told today unless we get something soon we might as well shut up shop ourselves. Very well, you'll go at once. Thank you. You'll ring as soon as you know." He flung the phone down and smiled at Michael.

"Stupid bastard. What he doesn't realise is that if my hunch fails to come off he'll very soon have no police station left."

He pulled open a drawer in the desk and brought out a flat leather-bound case.

"Well, boy, nothing to do for a moment, I think, just a question of waiting for Florrie to get her list, so we might as well have a game." He unfolded the chess board and pushed it towards Michael.

"My turn for white, I think, and remember, I pay for lunch tomorrow if you can beat me." He moved his king's knight and leaned back with a look of utter contentment on his face.

He nearly made it. Michael's pieces were sadly depleted and his king left cowering and alone in the corner of the board, when there was a knock on the door and Kirk's secretary came briskly in with a sheaf of papers in her hand.

"Thank you, Florrie, you've been very quick. Too quick, another five minutes and I'd have knocked you for six, Mike. Mate in four moves, I fancy. Now, let's see what we have here."

Florrie smiled maternally at him. "I'm afraid some of it is very vague, sir. I put in everyone we've got. Sometimes there's nothing more suspicious than the odd trip to Germany before the war."

"Good, that's exactly what I wanted. Our man wouldn't have been blatant about his activities. Let's have a look see."

He picked up the papers and began to read.

"No, no. Nothing here, nothing at all. What have we on the other side? Ah, ha, yes." His hand rapped sharply on the desk. "Got you.

"Fair enough, quite good enough for what we need, I fancy. Listen, Mike. Grace, Peter. Born Avonmouth nineteen nought-one. M.D. nineteen twenty-four, Clare College, London. Post-graduate course in psychiatry and general psychological medicine, Leipzig, twenty-four to thirty. General practice in Rathbone St. London, from nineteen thirty to his taking up present appointment at the West Tynecastle Hospital for—lot more of that, but here's what matters.

"During his student days, Grace appears to have been an enthusiastic supporter of the National Socialist Movement and after returning to England spent most of his holidays in Germany. He is said to have been intimate with Captain Roehm until the latter's murder in nineteen thirty-four. From that date he seems to have lost all leanings towards Nazism and never visited Germany again.

" 'It is the opinion of this department that Grace's political interests were due to a purely temporary and youthful enthusiasm, and completely changed with his bitterness over the death of Roehm. He can now be regarded as a perfectly reliable element and no action should be taken against him.' That's the lot, all nicely sealed and signed by your excellent predecessor."

"So it was Grace. All the damn time. Grace." Michael frowned at the chess board. "It fits beautifully, he had all the means. Medical pass, ambulance, hospital facilities. Everything, and I never for one moment thought of him. If ever there seemed an honest John Citizen it was Dr. Grace.

"And you think that somewhere in that hospital he's got Glyde?"

"I think he's got something somewhere, Mike. Something

that's been causing all the trouble. Something that Vanek saw, and which had a hole in its hand. That's all, I think. Do one thing for me, Mike. Just give me a good kick up the arse, if I ever again trust a man looking like Mr. Pickwick. Ah, that should be Jackson now. Take it, will you?" Michael lifted his hand towards the ringing phone and then paused.

"If it checks, sir, if there was a telegram, should I tell him to bring them in?"

"Oh no, boy. Not a bit of it. I don't want any big police boots clumping in there disturbing this bird. We'll attend to it ourselves just as soon as we're ready. Besides, after all these years I'm very interested in having a look at Mr. John Glyde. Take it, Mike."

"Hullo, oh yes, Inspector, Howard here." Michael spoke very quietly into the phone. "Yes, I know all about that. So there was a telegram all right. I see, it was delivered there on the third. It was sent from Berlin and addressed to the doctor personally, eh. Have they any recollection of the message? Pity, still, that should be enough. No, we've nothing to tell you yet. Many thanks." He glanced at Kirk and at his nod, replaced the phone.

"Right, that's it." Kirk got up and turned to Florrie. "Go and tell Willis I want the car in ten minutes, and you might be good enough to put some sandwiches and a flask of coffee in the back. Good girl." He walked to a cupboard and took out a heavy top coat.

"All right, this is it. It's all there. Vanek saw something in that hospital. He went to Germany to check on it. He made his appointment and died. He died because he was as big a fool as I was and sent a cable to Dr. Pickwick Grace and confided in him." He very carefully wrapped his coat around him and then added a grey woollen scarf.

"Better wrap up well, Mike. Gets very cold at night up there. No sense in getting a chill." He took something from the top of the cupboard and squinted at it. It was a heavy automatic pistol, and he handed it to Michael.

"Don't suppose we'll need this damn thing, but might as well take it along. I know you feel half dressed without it, don't you? Come on then, boy."

He carefully switched off the light and the fire and hurried out of the room to the lift.

"How far is it to Tynecastle, anyway? About two hundred miles, eh. About six o'clock now. Should get there by about eleven, if that old woman Willis can be made to keep his foot down. Just about right. I've always heard that we're supposed to be at our lowest ebb before the witching hour. Catch the blighter then, if we can."

They walked out of the lift across the gloomy hall and five minutes later were driving out through the theatre rush of West London.

CHAPTER FOURTEEN

At exactly five forty-five Penny walked out through the swing doors of the Mitre Hotel, Tynecastle, and got into the car. She had made good time on the journey up and left herself a full thirty minutes for a wash and a snack. Now she felt terrific, and hummed quietly to herself as the car rattled over the cobbles of the bridge and turned into the dark narrow streets of Gatesend. She drove slowly. There had been a football match in the town that afternoon and at each corner groups of a grey, cloth-capped army spilled into the roadway. It was already dusk with a thin mist beginning to rise from the river, and the street lamps glowing like phosphorous oranges in the damp air, as she crawled behind a tram, lurching ship-like up the hill.

Redfern Row was right at the top of the hill, almost out of the town where the smoke blackened Victorian buildings had begun to give way to Edwardian brick. It had an air of sham gentility and a hint of better days. It was just a sham though, it was all too near and too small. The thin layer of a sandwich wedged between squalor. In front were the rows of black terrace houses, the pubs, the fish shops and the football crowds, while behind lay the torn countryside with the pit heaps rising like mountains in the cinderstrewn fields.

She found the Stone House Café without difficulty. It was fake period, with a lot of beams and an air of concealing massive steel girders to support them. As she pushed open the door, a rather ecclesiastical-sounding bell tinkled in the back. It was like something out of a Catholic service before the crux of the Mass.

"Good evening, good evening." The man came hurrying out from behind a glass bead curtain. He was very tall, and completely studied in his part. If mannerisms impressed publishers, they would have been fighting for his contract long ago. He might have spent years looking at the pictures of authors on dust jackets and taking on a little part of all of them. Now he was firm and manly with hair brushed back, in a strong suggestion of Richard Aldington, with a touch of Graves.

"Good evening, have you come to join us, Miss—Miss—" he laughed boyishly.

"Mrs. Wise." Penny took his firm, manly hand. "I'd like to come to your meeting very much if I may, Mr. Aldington.—Oh, I beg your pardon, I'm afraid I don't know your name."

"Fenwick, Peter Fenwick. I suppose I do look a bit like Dickey Aldington," he said. He looked pleased as he said it, and Mr. Graves turned morosely away.

"Well, if you'd just sign the book and pay your bob for coffee, we'd be delighted to have you with us. Thank you so much." He pocketed the coin and peered at her signature.

"I say, that's great fun. Penny Wise, eh. Excellent. Mind if I make a note of it. I might be able to use it for my next effort." He pulled out a notebook and made his note. "There we are, Penny Wise, Pound Foolish." His laugh was short-lived beneath her bleak stare.

"Well, do come up, Mrs. Wise, and meet the boys and girls. We have the upstairs room these days." With the air of Mr. Aldington showing Georgette Heyer around his Pyreneen house, he held back the glass beads and waved her through.

There were about twenty boys and girls in the room upstairs. Penny was introduced to them in turn as a new arrival in the neighbourhood and a budding poetess. She bowed humbly to Mrs. Brocker, the President of the Society, magnificent in black and red satin, was honoured by a limp handshake from Mr. Edmund Cowdor, the author of "Untimely Ripped", and at the end of the line came to a tiny mouse-like creature who peered at her fearfully through spectacles, Miss Shirley Newton. Then Fenwick rang a bell and the West Gatesend Literary Group plunged into its activities.

And they were pretty discouraging. Mrs. Brocker read a dull and interminably long ode in honour of her father, a local magistrate. A stout and rather breathless girl gave a humourless sketch which was to be duly submitted to *Thompson's Weekly* after criticism by the Great Mr. Cowdor. It was criticised, in good round terms. Penny hoped Thompson would prove kinder.

After a coffee break came the final treat of the evening. A short story by Fenwick, which she distinctly remembered having read in a library book. "Saki Munro, H.H. Collected Short Stories of," the slip had informed her. It was just on nine when Mrs. Brocker pushed back her chair, thanked everyone for their presence, gave the highlights of next week's meeting and the group broke up.

Penny stood in the lower room talking to Fenwick, or making a pretence of talking, as the members collected hats and coats and streeled out into the road. Her eyes kept glancing away from him towards the door of the ladies' cloakroom, where Miss Newton was certainly taking her time.

"And you write verse, my dear, good, very good. A difficult and lonely calling, though." Fenwick raised his hand languidly to his hair and for a moment Aldington vanished and it was the Boy Chatterton who smiled sadly at her. Only for a moment though. "Personally I've always felt the novel was my particular vocation," he said as Aldington came back with a bang. "Difficult though. Still difficult to secure recognition in these days of control by the herd. That's why I think our little gatherings here are so important for anyone who is unwilling to prostitute their art. I do hope we will see you again, Mrs. Wise. Good night, Miss Newton." His voice dropped in key as the tiny creature came towards them.

"Oh, good night, Mr. Fenwick. I did so enjoy your reading. Really excellent."

"Thank you so much. Good night." He raised his eyebrows at Penny as the door closed behind her. "Praise indeed! Oh, I say, are you going? I was hoping that after I've locked up we might have a coffee together, there's quite a decent little place round the corner."

"Thank you so much, Mr. Fenwick. Sometime, I love that, but I see the fog's coming up and I'd better go. Good night." She withdrew her hand from his clasp and hurried to the door.

And the fog was thick. In both directions it lay like smoke in the road, with here and there an amber tinge as street lamps and lighted windows failed to pierce it. Penny stood on the pavement for a moment, irresolute of which direction to take and then walked quickly to the right as she heard a click of small footsteps hurrying away from her.

"Miss Newton, can I speak to you a minute?" She reached her just by the circle of a lamp. Under the red glow of neon tubes, her face looked oddly green.

"But of course, it's Mrs. Wise, isn't it, we were introduced at the Circle. I do hope you enjoyed the evening."

"Yes, very much, though I'm so sorry you didn't read."

"I, oh, I'm afraid I'm not very good, you know. I so much prefer to listen to Mrs. Brocker and Mr. Fenwick. One can learn so much from them I feel. Mr. Fenwick is really most professional, don't you think?"

"Miss Newton, it's you I want to talk about. I read about your story 'Playing with Fire' in the local paper, the plot interested me very much. I wonder if we could have a chat." She fumbled in her bag and brought out Poppy Murdock's Press card. "This is my professional name."

"Miss Murdock. *Woman's Sunday Gazette.*" She read it with difficulty in the hazy light. "But this is a London paper, Mrs. Wise. Whatever interest can my little story have for you?"

"We're going to do a series of articles upon the occult in literature, Miss Newton. You said the story just seemed to come to you, I'm wondering if we could use it." She pulled her coat tighter around her. "Perhaps we could have a cup of coffee together. Mr. Fenwick said there was a place nearby."

"Oh yes, there is, The Dairymaid. It's at the end of the road, but I don't think I'd better. It's after nine already and my landlady is getting on, she hates me to be out late at night." She looked at the card again and handed it back to Penny. "Perhaps you would come back with me to my room, Mrs. Wise. I've got a gas fire and I can easily make you a cup of tea. It's just around the corner." She smiled suddenly and somehow became rather appealing. "Do say yes, Mrs. Wise, it will be such fun for me to have a guest. Oh, good, it's not far." She moved on quickly with Penny at her side.

The house was very old and smelt of greens and cat. There were naked light bulbs and brown, very worn linoleum on the stairs. Behind a door in the hall, a gramophone played a modern rendering of an old-time dance tune.

"Do come in, Mrs. Wise. I'm afraid it's not very much, but as you know it's so difficult to get anything at all at a reasonable rent these days." She slipped a latch key into a third floor door and switched on the light.

The room wasn't much. There was the usual furnished letting middle-aged furniture. A strip of carpet on the stained floor and a narrow divan in the corner. Only a couple of water colours over the fireplace and one or two china ornaments seemed to have any of Miss Newton's personality about them.

"Do sit down, my dear. I think that is the better chair." She dropped on her knees and put a match to the gas fire. It flickered sadly and hummed through its cracked burners.

"I wonder, I wonder if while I make the tea if you'd like to have a glance at the story. It's very short and it won't take you long. Thank you so much." She slipped off her coat and took a thin pile of manuscript from a drawer. Once again Penny noticed that she had on a blue skirt and a blazer type jacket. They would have looked suitable on a schoolgirl of fifteen.

"Here you are, dear. Now do read it quickly and be as rude as you like about it. I'm sure it's of no importance and very badly written." She thrust the pages into Penny's hand and hurried out of the room.

It was badly written. Not only in style, which was flowery and tedious, but the very physical deciphering of the sprawling hand-writing was difficult.

If she had been a mistress in the junior department of a Grammar school, Penny would have given Miss Newton about four out of ten.

It was all there, though. The face that looked at her. The young, rather handsome face, that told her what to do. The hand with a hole in it which lay on some dark material and from time to time was lifted to the face and slowly drawn across the eyebrows. Penny stiffened as she read that. From a far off childhood memory she seemed to remember John making just that gesture.

By the time she put down the final page she was almost convinced that she was on to something at last.

"Here we are, my dear, do you take sugar?" Miss Newton fussed beside her with a tray. "Good, two lumps, here you are." She settled herself on a much rubbed leather hassock at the other side of the fire and looked anxiously at Penny. "Well, what do you think of it. I'm afraid it must seem very amateurish to you."

"Not a bit, Miss Newton. I was really quite fascinated." Penny spoke the literal truth. "We might be able to use it, but I wonder if you could tell me a bit more of how you came to write such a sinister story."

"I don't know, my dear. As I said at the Group, it just seemed to come on its own. I suppose since I've been an orphan—" she broke off for a moment, and although she was at least forty, the word was not completely ridiculous.

"Go on, Miss Newton, what happened when you became an orphan?"

"Well, I became a bit odd, Mrs. Wise. Mother died just over two years ago, you see, and with the debts I had to sell up our home and move into this room. I was very lonely, it's difficult at my age to make new friends, you see, and mother and I had always been so close together. I needed her so much, you see, that at last I—" She broke off and her lips trembled.

"What did you do, Miss Newton? You've no need to be embarrassed about anything in front of me."

"No, of course not, dear. You see, we've always been brought up in the Church of England and that kind of thing was very repugnant to us, but because I missed Mother, I began to get interested in Spiritualism."

She took a sip of tea before going on, and as she watched her, Penny suddenly knew that the woman was desperately frightened.

"Yes, I'm afraid I even went to a medium in Tynecastle. She was just a charlatan, of course. A blowsy old woman who smelt of alcohol. I didn't go again, but I read a lot about it. I read Sir Oliver Lodge and Mr. Tyrell, and everything the public library had on the subject. Then after a time, I began to get these dreams about that young man. Please don't think I'm insane but they were so real and he was so comforting. He told me that I could have Mother back. I could go to her any time I wanted, there was only one thing I had to do first."

She turned her face away from Penny for a moment.

"What did he want you to do?"

"Oh no, my dear, you don't understand. It wasn't him, he didn't want anything, he was just the go-between. It was Mother. You see, when she was ill, she was attended by Dr. McLeod. That was our local doctor. She knew now that the doctor had made a mistake. He had used the wrong treatment, if he hadn't made that mistake, she would still be alive. It was the same as murder, the young man said. And I," her voice dropped very low, "I was to avenge her, Mrs. Wise."

So that was how it was done. That was the pressure. Everything Michael and Kirk had told her came clicking together in a rush, and fitted. Just grant the possibility of telepathy and it was simple and logical. And this pale, trembling creature in front of her was the only one strong enough to get away.

She looked at Miss Newton with added respect.

"Revenge, I see. I know what you had to do. You had to kill the doctor, hadn't you. He told you to do that, didn't he? There was also something else, wasn't there. Go on, Miss Newton, tell me what was the other thing you were to do."

"You know, don't you, Mrs. Wise. You understand everything. There was something else I had to do, but I wasn't told at first. I would like to tell you about it, because it's such a comfort to talk to somebody. I wrote the story to try and get it off my chest, but it didn't do any good. No good at all." There were tears in her faded eyes now.

"Go on, talk to me then, Miss Newton. It's all right, because you didn't kill Dr. McLeod, did you?"

"Oh no, I couldn't when it came to the point, but you know I tried to. I bought poison, I told the chemist it was for green fly. I sent for the doctor to look at my arthritis. When he came, I made him a cup of tea. I was going to put the poison in the cup, when suddenly I knew what the other thing was that I must do, and that told me at once that it was an evil force which was speaking to me, not Mother. I put the poison down the drain as soon as Dr. McLeod left. But you, how do you know?"

"Don't worry about that, Miss Newton, you are all right, you got away. To you, suicide was the one unforgivable sin, so you saw the truth and got away. Now look at this, and tell me if you can recognise it." She reached in her bag and handed her a slip of paste-board.

"Miss Murdock, Mrs. Wise." The small face seemed to swell, break apart and die. "I don't know who you are. You may be anybody, but please, please tell me what I should do. I bought poison for the doctor, I nearly killed him and myself. And you know everything, because this—" The photograph slipped from her fingers and dropped to the floor. "This is the same face I saw in the dream."

"Yes, that is the face. Now I want to know something else. Where was the face? You describe it in the story as lying on some material in an enclosed space. Try and remember, Miss Newton, where was that space?"

"But that's easy, Mrs. Wise. I had to get to it always in the dream. There was a building, it was red brick, I think, and at the top of a hill. I've seen it before somewhere. I used to go in and walk down a long corridor, it was very brightly lit and smelt of antiseptic. If you take the last door on the right there is a staircase going down. A long way down. There was a locked door at the bottom of the stairs. I knew it was locked, but it didn't matter because I seemed to pass straight through it. At the far end of that room there was a little door. Just to the right of a desk. If you open that door and look down, far down, you can see the face. Now Mrs. Wise, please, please tell me what I should do. I daren't even sleep any more in case that dream comes back."

"I don't know, I quite honestly don't know." Penny stood up and reached for her bag. "Go to the police, go to a doctor, a priest. They'll all tell you much better than I can. All I can say is this. You did very, very well in resisting it, and even if you hadn't, even if you had done exactly as you were told, you would have been no more responsible for your actions than this door is for opening." She pulled it back and with a last look at the dingy room, the water colours, the hissing fire and the tiny, frightened creature who crouched over it, she walked quickly down the stairs.

It took her a good five minutes to find the car. The fog was a thick, acid blanket now, and each street seemed identical. It was with relief that she at last climbed into the Riley and switched on the comforting glow of the dashboard lights.

She was quite sure what she had to do and it had nothing to do with duty. Her duty was obvious. She should ring up Kirk or drive to the nearest police station and tell them what she had heard. But she was past all idea of duty now. She believed she was at last at the end of her trail. Just let her find the place that Miss Newton had described and she would be where she wanted. She turned on the engine and then leaned out as footsteps came through the fog towards her.

The policeman was six foot three and his cape made his shoulders look enormous. He bent down and grinned at her.

"Ullo, Miss," he said. "You got lost in this ruddy mist?"

"No, not yet, officer, though I probably soon will be. What I want is a bit of information from you."

"Information. Surely, if I can, Miss." He settled himself more comfortably against the side of the car, glad of any break in the boredom of his patrol. "And what information would you be wanting?"

"I want to know about a building, officer. It sounds crazy, but I don't know its name, or even where it is, just the description. It's a big red brick building and it stands on the top of a hill somewhere. Could be a hospital or something like that. Probably near here, but not too near."

"I see, big red brick place on the top of a hill, near here." He thought for a moment. "Kind of hospital or something. That could cut it down a bit. The St. John's is brick, but it's not on a hill. The General's on a hill but it's stone. Outside the town, you say, Miss. It couldn't be that mental place at Wandswick, could it? That fits your description."

"It could indeed, officer. It almost certainly is. How do I get there?"

"Well, it's a bit involved like, and with this fog you're going to 'ave the devil of a job. You've got to follow the road to the station, get over the bridge and then take the main road on the right. About a mile and a half along that, and you'll come to it. See the gates on the right, top of the only real hill you come to. If I was you, I'd put it off till tomorrow, though."

"But I'm not, am I, officer, I do wish I was, but I'm sorry I'm not. Goodnight, officer, and thanks a lot."

Penny waited for him to draw back and then slammed the Riley into gear and, as fast as the fog allowed, drove off in the direction he had indicated. She didn't get far. About half a mile down the curtained street, her foot came down hard on the brake pedal.

"Glory, glory Hallelujah, Glory, glory Hallelujah, for his soul goes—Damn you."

The singing drunks staggered out of the fog in front of her and her long bonnet was within an inch of touching them. They lurched sideways and one of them spat. Then, troll-like they vanished into the thick air and only their voices remained, dull and tuneless, but still defiant in the chorus of the march.

'We'll hang Jeff Davis on a sour apple tree.
 We'll hang Jeff Davis on a sour apple tree.
 We'll hang Jeff Davis on a—'

"Yes, on a sour apple tree." Penny listened as the voices and the shambling footsteps died and once more she was alone in the warm, secure car with only her thoughts to trouble her. But the drunks were right. They were dead right, for that was it. "We'll hang Jeff Davis on a sour apple tree." That went right in the centre of the target, because it was a tree. John was like a tree. A blighted tree with his roots and branches stretching out into the soil and the sky, and the sour sap running through them to blast everything they touched. A family tree. The tree of John and her father, who had faced nothing, and, yes, she herself. The last, little bud thrown from the topmost branch of the 'sour apple tree.' And now she was going back to it. Back home, on family business.

'And his soul goes marching on.'

The last drunken notes wafted down to her, and suddenly she needed a drink, too. She reached in the car pocket and pulled out the flask that Tony Field always kept there.

She took a long drink and then drove on. "And here's to Jefferson Davis," said Penny Glyde.

CHAPTER FIFTEEN

It was a long, dull drive to the North and the fog made it longer. Kirk kept the windows tightly closed and with his cigar smoke, the atmosphere in the car became as thick as the fog outside. From time to time he glanced at his watch, and swore at the driver to hurry. It was just after eleven when they pulled up the hill and saw the hospital lights blinking above them.

"Well, Mike, this seems to be it. The end of the line, but all the same, we're going to take things very easy with him at first. Just be gentle and sweet and try to get him to talk. No suicides this time, any suspicion of that and you lay him out cold. Understood?"

"Yes, sir, I understand." Michael fingered the handle of his Luger and then pushed open the door as the car slid to a halt across the gravel. There was a porter looking at them from the top of the short flight of steps.

Kirk didn't hurry. He yawned, stretched and for a moment looked around him as if uncertain as to where he was. Then he dropped his cigar, ground it carefully out on the gravel and began to walk up the steps.

"Good evening, Porter." His voice was pleasant and cheerful. "I believe that Dr. Grace has a flat in the hospital, would you please direct us there?"

"Well, sir, I don't think the doctor will be in the flat." He glanced at the clock over the door. "He left a note that he'd be working right through till midnight. Said he wasn't to be disturbed. I could ring through to his office, of course, and find out if he'll see you. Was he expecting you, gentlemen?"

"No, he wasn't expecting us, Porter, but it's all right, we know where the doctor's office is and we'll find our own way. Don't you bother to ring, just get on with whatever you were doing."

"Well, I don't know, sir." The man started to protest, but something in Kirk's eyes stopped him. "Very good, gentlemen, as you say." He turned and went back into his office. There was a Western on the telephone switchboard, he picked it up as he sat down and began to read.

The corridor seemed endless, and the white ceiling lamps gave it the suggestion of an underground subway; there could have been little winking panels on the walls, 'Follow the Blue Light to Piccadilly.'

At each step, Michael felt a jab of uncertainty. Not uncertainty that this was the end. That was all clear now. It all tied up and the facts fitted too closely to be coincidence. At any moment they would open Grace's door, and they would be with the man who knew, the prime mover. But what lay behind him? What was the thing that Three Sixes had brought from Bergen? There was a quick ticking pulse in his forehead as, at last, Kirk stopped and knocked at a door marked 'Principal, Private.'

"Come in, come in." Grace's voice, as hearty and self-confident as ever, rang through the hardboard. Kirk turned the handle and they stepped out of the gleaming corridor into the dark, trophy-hung room.

"Well, who is it? What do you want?" Grace sat at his desk under a shaded lamp which gave a greenish tinge to his bald head. He was turning over some papers and he didn't look up at once.

"Good evening, Dr. Grace." Kirk's voice was bland and cheerful. "Very sorry to have to barge in on you at this hour, but I think it's time we had another little chat."

"General Kirk! What on earth can you want. Why, it's past eleven." Grace got up from his chair and looked dazedly at them.

"Sorry, General, very sorry, forgetting my manners. This wretched business has been getting me down lately. Do find yourselves a couple of chairs." He sank back and turned up the light shade.

"Well, any news? The rate is still mounting, isn't it? We must find something soon, you know. I feel almost personally responsible for the whole thing. I mean, it starting here in a way."

"Yes, in a way it did start here, didn't it. That's why I know that you'll want to help us." Kirk beamed at him, and Michael was suddenly reminded of a big cat creeping towards its prey.

"But of course, anything I can do, anything at all."

"Good. It's very little really, just a simple question. As you will have heard from your colleague Dr. Reade, we learnt quite a lot from Professor Ranier. We have now an inkling as to how and why the thing works. It only remains to find the where. I hope you may be able to help us on that point, Dr. Grace."

"I? But I don't understand. After all, it's outside my province. I'm merely a medical man, not a detective."

"So you are, doctor. But I still think you can help us. Let us imagine, for a moment, that our present theory is correct. Let us suppose that something which was once called Glyde was landed from a U-boat on the Scottish coast. Then what? What would become of it? Where could it be hidden? Have you any ideas on that point, Dr. Grace?"

"I don't know. They had their regular agents, I suppose."

"Oh, yes, they had their regular agents, but they didn't use them in this case. No regular agent could have fitted that bill. Besides by that date, I think I'd got them all." Once more he smiled and the cat was very near the bird, now. "No, Doctor, they wanted another kind of person. Somebody above suspicion. Somebody with special facilities who had been kept back for just such an emergency. Somebody with means of both transport and storage. Tell me, doctor, just where were you on the second of May, nineteen forty-five?"

"Where was I? But this is absurd, General Kirk. How can I remember? I was here, I suppose, but I can't be sure, after all these years."

"But I think you can remember, Doctor. I don't imagine you'll ever forget that trip to Scotland and the thing you brought back with you." Kirk's voice suddenly hardened. "No, Doctor, not that way. Don't try it that way." Grace was almost on his feet now. Crouched like the letter S, he bent over the desk and reached for something. It was a small capsule and it looked like a bead in the green light.

"Put it down, Doctor, I'm not having any more of that. If you lift it another inch towards your mouth, Mr. Howard will blow your hand off."

Michael held the automatic tight against his side and his finger was on the trigger as he waited. He never used it. For a long moment Grace crouched quite still, looking at him. Then his hand opened and the capsule rolled to the floor. When he stood up, his chest was heaving and something started to happen to his face.

"Yes, you're—you're right, General—quite right." The words came gasping out of his big chest. "I did it. I met the submarine and I brought him here, but I never, I never thought, never—" Like a backcloth parting, Mr. Pickwick walked out of his face and it became drawn and frightened and old; terribly old. Not old with any pleasant maturity, but just old with the dreadful age of despair.

"—I never thought it would be like that." The words were torn from him, and he seemed to be trying to speak from a long way off from under water.

"—I never thought, so please, General Kirk, please—help—me—" His voice slipped away to nothing and at the same moment all expression was wiped off his face. Then he slumped back into the chair, motionless.

"Damn, I think he's gone." Kirk bent over him and picked up his wrist. "I can't feel a thing. Did you see him take anything, Mike?"

"Not a thing, sir. I was watching him all the time. He just seemed to crumple up."

"Well, he's out now. No heartbeat that I can feel." He tilted the lamp over the still face and pulled back an eyelid. "Doesn't seem to be any reaction to light either. I think he's had it, but go and fetch a doctor. Damn it all, this is a hospital, they may be able to do something."

"That will not be necessary, General Kirk, I am a doctor." In their excitement, neither of them had noticed that Reade had come into the room. She put down the papers she was carrying and crossed to Grace. She was like a governess finding a brawl at a children's party, as competent and unruffled as ever.

"I see." Her examination was very quick. "This man is dead. May I ask you exactly what happened?"

"I don't know. We were talking and suddenly he seemed to collapse. Could it have been a stroke?"

"A stroke. Yes, I suppose you might just call it that. Tell me,

General. Before it happened. What were you talking about before he, as you say, collapsed?" She looked at Kirk and there was something about her that he had not seen before. She was still firm and confident and reassuring, but she was strangely different.

"I asked him a certain question, Doctor. A question of the utmost importance. You see, I think I now know what happened. I think it was Grace who met that U-boat."

"I see, and when you asked him that he died. Perhaps you were right. In any case, I think it's time we all looked at Dr. Grace's private possessions." She bent down and, taking a key from the dead man's pocket, crossed to the door in the corner of the room. There was a light behind it which showed a flight of steps running down.

"Come with me, gentlemen, I am quite sure we will find it interesting." She walked through the doorway and motioned them to follow her.

There were fifteen steps down to the basement room and it was bright and cheerful. There were pink, shaded lights around the walls and the steel chairs had tartan covers; on the corner desk there was a vase of flowers. Apart from the chairs and the desk, the room was bare of furniture. At the back there was a steel trolley heaped with shining instruments, and just to the right of it stood three steel cylinders. They hissed slightly and rubber tubes led from them and vanished through a hole in the wall.

Reade crossed to the cylinders and glanced briefly at the gauges on top of them.

"Sit down, please, gentlemen, and make yourselves comfortable for a moment." She leaned against the desk and smiled. She was like a school teacher giving a private class to two backward pupils.

"You know quite a lot now, don't you, General, quite a lot. Still I think there are one or two things I can tell you. But first, tell me something. Tell me about Grace. Who do you think he really was?"

Kirk didn't answer her for a moment. He sat very still and looked at her and all at once he knew why she was different. He looked at her white hair and saw that it was oddly coarse and masculine. He looked at her hands and saw that they were red and powerful. He looked at her face and though it had the same expression of quiet authority it was a different kind of authority now. Now, no longer the authority of the school room, the governess, but of the jailer. Like an efficient calculating machine his mind fitted the pieces together and he knew who he was talking to. But all the same he would play it her way. Whatever happened he had to play it her way.

"I think that Grace was one of the prime movers in this business, Dr. Reade. I think he was an English-born Nazi collaborator, and it was he who went to Spey Inlet and met the party from the submarine. I think that all these years he has been hiding something here in this hospital. I also think that you know what that thing is. Now, what is it you were going to show us?"

"All in good time, General. I will show you what you want to see, but first, I would like a cigarette. Thank you, Mr. Howard." She inhaled deeply and pulled herself up on to the flap of the desk.

"Now, gentlemen, you've done very well so far, and you're right in one way. Grace did meet the U-boat. He did bring something back with him. He did hide it here, but he had no idea of what it was." She smiled suddenly and there was nothing nice about her smile.

"Just now. General Kirk, you described Grace as a prime mover, that is where you are wrong, completely wrong. You'll never know just how wrong you were. You see, Grace never moved anything, he was merely a dummy, moved by the thing he was sent to collect. He got his message to go to Spey Inlet, he took an ambulance with him and it all went very smoothly, but they never told him what that U-boat was bringing. And once he had it, once he had brought it here, he became completely absorbed by the thing he had hidden. No, General Kirk, Grace was never the prime mover, only a puppet. Now do you understand?"

"Yes, Dr. Reade, now I understand." Kirk looked at her face and the shadow behind the face and he had no doubts left. Like Grace, this woman too was just the servant of the thing she had fed and harboured and—yes, that too. The thing she had made.

"You know," he said, "I think it's time you told me who you are, madam."

"You mean you don't know, you still aren't sure about that, but you just think my name may not be Reade. You're right, of course. There was a Reade, but it seems she died." Her eyes flicked away from him and she looked at Michael.

"Do take your hand out of your pocket, Mr. Howard. It is quite unnecessary and looks most ridiculous."

"Yes, quite unnecessary, Mike, take these instead." Kirk reached in his overcoat. The handcuffs glinted dully in the pink light.

"I think this is the end now, isn't it, madam? It should have been much earlier, but I missed two little pieces of information.

"You see, we always thought that someone had died in the Herford bombing, and we were wrong. That was the first slip, and the second was even more trivial, yet more vital in a way. It was just one little blur we got in the report from Germany, yet it makes all the difference. Just the spelling of a name. Yes, Doctor, for lack of a shoe the kingdom was lost. For lack of a letter, we almost lost. Just one letter. Just 'A', the first little letter of the alphabet, that at times makes so much difference to both sense and gender." He reached over and passed the handcuffs to Michael.

"It was you, wasn't it, whom Grace fetched from Scotland and you had someone with you? Correct me if I'm wrong, Number 666.

"Very well, Mike. Would you be good enough to arrest Frau Doktor Erika Rhine."

Michael moved towards her and then stopped dead as she laughed. She laughed, but her action had nothing to do with the conventional meaning of the word. Nothing at all. It was not mirth or humour or joy, just air shaking in her lungs and lips, but as she laughed he looked into her face and for an instant saw the terrible space behind the eyes.

"I beg your pardon." The laughter ceased as if cut off by a tap, and she held out her hands. "That was extremely rude of me. Please put your handcuffs on if you wish, Mr. Howard. But before you do that, aren't you curious? Don't you want to see what really happened?"

Her left hand slid down on to the desk and she pressed a switch. On the wall by the cylinders a panel slid open like a camera shutter.

"Go on, Mr. Howard. I promised I would show you something very interesting. There's nothing to hurt you, so go to the wall and look down. Look down." Once more came the mirthless choking laugh.

"Look down and behold the Man."

"Get back, Mike. Get away from that wall." Kirk stepped towards him and his voice was harsh and urgent. "Get back, damn you. We don't know what's down there yet."

But he was too late. Michael had already moved forward and was peering down through the open panel. For a moment he seemed to stand quite naturally, and then his body went stiff. He turned round and took two paces forward and looked at Kirk. There was something in his face that had not been there before.

It took Penny a long time to find the hospital. For hours she seemed to blunder about in the dark fog-bound streets of the town, running into squares and cul-de-sacs with surprising regularity. She was very tired when at last she found the main road and saw the lights of the building on the hill top.

The fog had lifted a little. She could see the curve of the drive, between the trees and the lighted doorway. There was a big car drawn up before the steps.

She pulled the Riley on to the verge a few yards before the gates and switched off the lights. Then she lit a cigarette and tried to relax. She had to think before she went blundering through the entrance. If that woman's story was true, and she was quite sure it was, then everything she wanted to know was inside that building. Somewhere in a room below the ground. The last door on the right at the end of the passage, and there were steps running down to a door that was locked. Well, she would have to deal with that obstacle when she came to it. The first thing was to get into the building.

She got out, threw away her cigarette and took a dark coat from the boot of the car. Then she started to walk through the gates towards the entrance.

She kept on the grass verge of the drive where the shrubs gave her a bit of cover and her feet made no noise. Very soon she was beside the parked car. There was something about it that was vaguely familiar, but she didn't pay much attention. The important thing was the driver. He was leaning far back against the cushions with his mouth open, and quite obviously fast asleep. She skirted round the car and paused for a moment before the five steps that led up to the entrance of the hospital.

There were two ways of doing it. In the little glass box at the top of the steps she could see the porter. He was sitting on a chair with his back to the light and the door, and he had a book in his hand. He looked pretty comfortable and settled. Two ways. She could either brazen it out. March straight up to him and demand to see the Director; what was the name Michael had told her? Yes, Grace. If she said that she knew where to find him the chances were that the man might return to his novel and let her go alone. The second way was to try and creep past him and get into that passage without being seen. She would compromise. Try the second way and if seen, then go back to the first. She blessed the flat, rubber-soled shoes she used for driving and walked up the steps as quietly as she could, but without any air of trying to gain a furtive entrance.

It worked beautifully. Not for one flicker of a second did the porter look around. He was completely glued to the book and seemed to read with difficulty. Penny could see his finger following the line of print and his lips moving as he read each word. She went past the box, keeping the big hall lamp between them, and the next moment was through the frosted glass doors into the passage.

She went down it like a ghost. The floor was of some rubber composition and her shoes made no sound. Far away at the end of the long row of lights she could see two doors facing her. The one on the right, Miss Newton had said. Not far now, her heart pounded with excitement as she walked towards that innocent-looking door.

"Good evening, can I help you at all?" The nurse came quickly out of an adjoining passage and smiled at her. She had her cape on and was obviously just going off duty.

"No, it's all right, Sister, thank you. The porter told me the way."

"Quite sure?" There was a fleeting glance of relief in the bright smile. "Good night, then." She turned on her heel and hurried on towards the entrance hall.

The door opened quietly and easily on well-oiled hinges. Inside it smelt strongly of polish and a faint hint of carbolic soap. She closed the door after her and fumbled for a light switch. She couldn't find one. The place seemed to be used as some kind of store by the cleaners. She touched the handle of a vacuum cleaner, and her toe rang sharply against a pail. Then she took the lighter out of her handbag and in its thin, blue flame saw a flight of steps leading down from the far end of the cupboard. So far, so good. So far Miss Newton had spoken the exact truth. Holding her lighter in front of her, she groped forward and down.

There were fifteen steps. Fifteen steep concrete ledges that felt oddly cold through her rubber shoes and at each step she heard a little whisper in her head.

"That's right, Penny," it said. "Just come as you're coming because this is the road home and I'm waiting for you. I'm waiting as I've always waited, so come on down the stairs and then we'll be together again and safe. Come on, Penny Glyde, put your hands in front of you and don't mind the dark. Just come forward and find me as you did when we played in the box-rooms together years ago. Come on, there's nothing to fear here. No rats or spiders or anything that can hurt you, so come on quickly. Come on, Penny, come on forward—to me—home—"

The whisper rose to a harsh urgency and then died as her hand came sharply against the barrier of a door. She shut her eyes for a moment and leaned against the wall. Then she lifted the lighter.

The door looked thick and impregnable and the shield of a patent lock glinted in the flame. From behind it she heard an indistinct murmur of voices. She turned the handle and pushed it forward. It moved the tenth of an inch before the lock held.

As she listened to the voices a terrible urgency came over Penny. It was not thought out, it was hardly mental. It was just a craving, a longing which made the opening of that door the one important thing in her life.

But how? In thrillers it was simple. Scores of characters seemed to walk to and from locked vaults with ease. But how was it done? Raffles carried a folder of patent keys in his pocket. Father Brown's reformed Frenchman used bent wire. Neither of these seemed to apply. Were cylinder locks invented in the days of Messrs. Hornung and Chesterton? No, possibly not. There was something else though. In a dull journey from Paris there had been a Roman Policier. The plot was completely faded from her memory, but there had been an incident like this. At the time she had doubted whether it would work, but it was worth a try. She opened her bag, and blessing all tradesmen, pulled out the thin cellulose calendar from the off-licence. It looked simple, but it had to be just right. There had to be enough of a gap between the door and the frame, then if you were careful and worked the stuff well home, the lock would move back. She folded the calendar in half, bent it slightly and pressed it into the crack.

"All right, John, I'm coming now," she said, as she felt it go home.

CHAPTER SIXTEEN

Michael Howard turned slowly and looked at Kirk. He seemed to see him as from a long way off and his features were blurred and indistinct.

He had not made out much of what had been behind the wall because as he had leaned forward to look down, something had happened to him, and now he was slowly sinking through the floor of the room to another time and another place.

For a time he couldn't make out where he was. It was dusk and he was lying down on something soft. In front of him he could see a pale moon through a casement window, and all around there was a creak of old furniture. He looked up and suddenly he knew. He was eight years old and he had just woken up out of the dream. He brought his hand from beneath the bedclothes to wipe the sweat from his forehead, and as he did so, he knew that everything was wrong.

It was the face that was wrong, of course. The face that was three yards away and looking at him. The face from the dream that had ended: that was the frightful thing. The dream had ended and it was still there. It came down a tube and it was the worst thing in the world. He had to try to turn from it, to block the tube and seal it up for ever, but it never worked that way. His body never responded and he had to lie still and watch it coming and pray he would wake before it reached him. But now he was awake, he was wide awake and the face was still there, looking at him. He turned his head and tried to think of a way to stop it, and as he did his hand felt something heavy at his side, and knew that there was a way. The gun was like a great comforting talisman in his hand. Just let that face come another yard nearer and he would stop it. He would have to stop it, though he dreaded what it might become as it vanished in red ruin before his eyes.

It was speaking to him now, but he wouldn't listen. If he listened it would come closer, and then—

He clutched the gun and turned it towards the face.

"Stop it, Mike. Pull yourself together and snap out of it."

Kirk's voice was like the crack of a whip. "Look at me, and pull yourself together and wake up. Go on, Mike. For God's sake do as I say. Snap out of it." He looked at the set, controlled face and despair as thick as the fog outside closed around him.

"You're wasting your time, General Kirk, there's nothing you can do any more, nothing at all, because Mr. Howard has now become one of us." Once more Rhine smiled her mirthless smile.

"You fool, General Kirk, you poor, bloody foolish fool. You thought you could come blundering in here, didn't you? You thought you could control it. You control it, when you have no conception at all of the power we have made. The power which started with one man and has become an army."

Kirk looked at her, and past her to the cylinders with their tubes running into the wall and he knew that there was still one slight chance left to him. It was a tiny, probably hopeless chance but he had to take it. Whatever its form, the thing behind the wall was a physical entity, and it needed those cylinders to live. If he could just get to them and turn off the supply, they might still win. He measured the distance he would have to go. Twelve feet perhaps; no, nearer fifteen, and the gun was pointing directly at him. Still, a good jump under the gun, a wrench at the tubes, and even if he was hit, the thing might weaken and Michael would come round and finish the business for him. There was just that one chance, and it had to be taken.

He braced himself against the chair, began to lean forward

with the soles of his shoes pressed hard on the floor, and at the same instant knew that he would never make it. He was too old. Twenty years ago, and it would have been easy. Fifteen years and it would have been all right. Ten years, and it might have just been all right. Now it was impossible. The stream of the years was like a shackle around his feet, a steel shackle tempered by too many whiskies, too many cigars, too many hours in his dark, overheated office. He knew quite clearly that he would be blasted by the automatic before he even left the chair.

"Try it that way if you like, General. I know what you're thinking, so go ahead and try it. I will be interested to see how far you get. About five feet, I imagine. Mr. Howard thinks you are something he was once very frightened of, and I don't imagine he would let you come any nearer." She swung round on the desk and opened one of the cylinder taps half a revolution.

"And now it's your turn, I think, General Kirk. You see, we all have some private fear or horror, and I wonder what yours may be. Very soon we will know. It's only just and fair, isn't it? You were the person who made us hurry, so now it will come to you. We were going to take our time, you see. Just wait until we were quite ready, but you stopped that, you and Vanek. That fool Vanek, who broke in here and saw a scar which had once been described to him and tried to make money out of it. Fortunately, like you, he thought Grace was the prime mover and he told me what he had seen, and that was the end of Mr. Vanek. Now it's your turn. I shall leave you alone with it for a little. Yes, you can feel it now, can't you, General Kirk?" She got up from the desk and went to the door, like a cool, white shadow.

And Kirk felt it. There was a noise of the sea in his head, and a whisper behind it, and the sea's waves were throbbing bars of pain. He gripped the steel arms of the chair and fought the waves. He had to fight them. Just let him listen to the voice behind, and the business was finished for ever. He clenched his teeth and fixed his eyes on the corner door, as each succeeding wave of pain wracked him like a probe in his skull.

Concentrate on the door, that was what he had to do. There was a scar of peeled paint below the lintel, so think about that. Think about its shape first. It was rather like a moth wasn't it? A moth with its wings spread open. Come on now, think, what was its size? Be exact, damn you. Yes, say an inch and a quarter across by three-quarters vertical.

God, but that one hurt him. Like leaded weights, the waves pounded in his head, and the knowledge that he could stop them made them worse. It was so easy. He had just to relax and listen to the voice and close his eyes and the pain would stop for ever.

No, fight it. Go on, fight it, you bastard. Fight it, you useless old bastard, who can't move quickly. Go on and fight it and try to earn your keep.

What was its colour, then? Blue, light blue. The same light, grey-blue that the council used on their office buildings. Oh, Lord, please make them stop. But what had caused it? How had it happened? Something had banged against it, and the painter couldn't have primed the surface properly, because in the tip of the right wing there was a speck that showed the brown hardboard behind the undercoat.

No, no, please no. He couldn't—he couldn't go on—no—please let it stop—he'd got to make it stop. He threw a last despairing glance at the chip of paint and prepared to accept the words in his head, when suddenly the pain died and his head was clear, as the door opened and through the door, blinking slightly in the pink light, came Penny Wise. He didn't believe it at first. It seemed so utterly impossible that he couldn't believe it. It was only when she closed the door behind her that he knew she was nothing to do with his imagination.

Penny stood quite still, for a moment, looking round the room, and her expression didn't alter. She looked at him and at Michael and the desk and the flowers on the desk, and there seemed to be nothing that interested her. She might have been blind for all the expression in her eyes. Then she saw the panel in the wall and very slowly she began to move towards it.

And suddenly Kirk knew that this was the end. Whichever way she went, it was the end. For better for worse, friend or enemy, whoever she was, she had to be the end. The one person who could save or finish them.

"Penny," he said. "Before you go to the panel. Before you go and look down and destroy yourself utterly, stop and listen to me."

Like a sleep-walker she turned and faced him, but there was no recognition in her eyes.

"Thank you," he said, and he put every atom of meaning into his voice. "Now, tell me. Which side are you on?"

"Side, which side?" It was not speech, but just a movement of her lips and words coming through them. "There's only one side, isn't there? His, and I must go to him."

"No, Penny, there are two sides. His and ours. His down there in the box, and ours. Ours, Penny. Yours and mine and Michael's. And Michael's, Penny. Look at him. Look at Mike, and then do as I say."

Her eyes flickered across the room, and for a moment her expression changed and became normal. "Mike," she said. "It is you, Mike. Please look at me. Please, please help me, Mike." She started to walk towards him as she spoke.

"No, Penny, not yet. Don't go to him yet. Mike's sick, he needs help too, and you're the only one who can give it. Now, do what I tell you. You see those cylinders by the wall. Go to them, and turn off the taps. Right, Penny, go to the cylinders and turn off the taps. Now, turn off the taps."

With his heart like a hammer in his chest he saw her cross the room and lift her hand. He prayed to every god who had ever moved him as he saw the first tap turn slightly. Then, like a puppet on a wire, she jerked sideways towards the panel, and all his hopes died.

Penny stood by the hole in the wall and she went quite rigid. He could see her fingers grow white as they gripped the edges and she looked down. For perhaps a minute she stood like that, quite motionless and then she started to speak.

"No," she said. "No, John, not like that. Not that. I didn't think it would be like that. I never guessed you could ever be like that."

But he was like that. He was just like that. That was the truth; that was what he had become. After all the years the story told and he was home again. He was back home in a lead-lined box with a smell of antiseptic and corruption and a little amber light revealing everything. Yes, everything. As some obscene, fairground exhibit, he lay on his back with the air roaring in his lungs like a broken winded horse on a hill, and the pierced hand clenching and unclenching over the grey tubes as they forced nourishment and life into every secret, private aperture of his terrible body.

All that and the face too. Above all the face. The face that was so changed but still remembered. Huge now in the swollen head which had absorbed its own bone structure and spread outwards till it dwarfed the rest of the body; with the same blue eyes she had watched years ago, staring up at her through the bursting sockets.

She turned away from the shutter and leaned back against the wall, her face working.

"No, John, it's no good now. You drew me to you, but you can't touch me any more. I never knew, you see. I never guessed what you were and now it's too late, far too late, and I'm going to stop you. Goodbye, John. This is the end, because I have to stop you. I'm the only one left to do it and, God help me, you're my responsibility; my sole responsibility."

She lifted her hand and grasped the tap again. She gave it one full turn and then looked up as the door in front of her opened.

She didn't look twice. There was no need for her to look twice. At the first glance at that heavy, white-haired face she knew her.

She left the tap and walked towards Rhine, seeing half her, and half the thing in the case, and horror gave way to rage as she walked.

"You," she said. "You did it, didn't you? You dared to do it. Oh, yes, I know he was bad, evil possibly, but you made him like that. You dared to do that to a human being; to my brother." She took a heavy, wooden ruler from the desk as she spoke.

"Don't. You're the sister, aren't you, so listen, please listen." The woman crouched against the side of the wall, drawing away from her, and as she spoke her voice began to alter. "Penny, you mustn't do it." The words became purely masculine and there was a drawl and a hint of Oxford about them. "Penny, try and understand. It's me, too." And then Penny hit her.

She hit her with everything she'd got. She hit her with the ruler and her fist and her feet. She drove her round the room, striking and kicking as she went. She threw her on the floor and hit her again as she tried to rise.

Rhine scrabbled on the floor and her face was no longer completely human. It was part male, part female and wholly horrible, with a glow in the eyes that seemed to come from outside itself.

Kirk sat in his chair with a great sense of impotence and he watched both her and Michael. For one moment he saw her pull herself away from Penny, and struggle to rise to her feet, with her hands like claws tearing in front of her. Then the heavy ruler came down across the side of her neck and she fell backwards across the cylinders.

The next moment Kirk was on his feet. As she fell, he saw the three cylinders topple forward under her weight, and the tubes pull away from their sockets as they moved. At the same instant the gun dropped from Michael's hand and he crumpled up on the floor. There was a loud hissing sound from the cylinder taps now, and from behind the panel, something moved.

Kirk knelt down and felt Michael's pulse. Then he looked at Penny.

"Well done, little lady. Quite a scrap. You all right?"

"Yes, yes, I'm all right. For the first time I'm all right." There was a long scratch down the side of her face and she was breathing heavily, but she could just manage a smile. Then she looked at Michael and threw herself down on the floor beside him.

"Mike, Mike, darling. Please look at me." She cradled his head in her arms and bent over him. A drop of blood fell from her face and ran down his cheek.

"Don't worry about your boy friend, he'll be all right." Kirk watched Michael open his eyes and smile at her. Then he turned to the woman by the cylinders. She was quite dead. Like Grace, she had only drawn her power from the thing she had made and when it left her, there was no alternative to death. For a moment he looked at the oddly wolfish face of the prime mover and then his head jerked round as Penny screamed.

She was kneeling beside Michael, shielding his head with her arm, and she was screaming at the top of her voice. He didn't need to know why; before he had looked past her at what she was staring at, he knew why. For the opening in the wall was no longer empty.

While he had been looking at the woman, the thing in the case had got up. It had got up, dying in its agony and lifted its face to the door of the tomb. Its huge face, swollen and distorted and scarlet now, as it struggled for what had fed it. Its face which was two feet across, filling the opening, with its blue eyes staring at them and its lips trying to move while one grey pipe still hung from them. And at last, with a gigantic effort, it did speak.

"I," it said. "I, I, I," it said. Over and over again it said just "I"; while the scarlet turned to purple and black and each vein glowed and burned and became a luminous pipe. Then the flesh swelled outwards till it pressed against the side of the wall, and at last with "I's" turning to a scream and a noise like tearing paper, the creature withered.

"Sorry, sir, terribly sorry. I just don't know what came over me." Michael sat in a deep chair in Grace's study, and with brandy, his colour was beginning to come back. "When I looked through that panel, something just seemed to hit me, and there wasn't a damn thing I could do to stop it. I can't remember anything till I was lying on the floor with Penny bending over me."

"And there wasn't anything you could do, Mike, so stop worrying. There's nothing at all to worry about. You see, you were no more to blame than I was. Another ten seconds and I'd have gone the same way. We've just got to thank our lucky stars that this young woman of yours got her hunch and turned up when she did. We owe the lot to her, and if anyone is to blame, I am. I thought we were both strong enough to resist it. I should have remembered what Ranier told us; that every minute that thing was growing in strength, and very soon it would not only be the unbalanced who were affected." Kirk put his glass down on the table and turned round as the door opened.

"Well, Inspector, everything all right now? Everything tidied up to your satisfaction at last?"

"More or less, sir. Pity they were both dead though. I'd have liked to have had one of them. Heart failure, you say it was?"

"Yes, we'd better put it down as heart failure. A nice, convenient term that. All a lie though. In this case it wasn't their hearts that failed, it was his."

"Yes, sir. Just as you say. Still, I would have liked one of them alive for the inquiry."

"I bet you would, old boy. It doesn't matter though. There'll be no inquiry. I'll take care of that." He glanced at a pile of typescript on the table. "We've got everything we want. This is Rhine's account of the whole business. It gives all the details, all the processes they went through. Localizing the brain centres they found and then using ultraviolet on them. They were doing fine, just fine, until—"

"Until what, sir?"

"Until it got out of hand and started to control them."

"I see, sir." The policeman looked dubiously at the papers. "Well, I think I'd best be getting along now. Still a lot of work to be done back at the station. Will you be staying here a little longer, General?"

"Yes, just a bit longer and then we're off back to London." He got up and held out his hand. "Goodbye, Inspector. Thanks for your help. I'll be writing in a day or two."

"Goodbye, sir." The man took his hand and then crossed to the door. When he had gone, Kirk turned to the window and looked out.

It was already day. The fog had blown away in the morning breeze and he could see the long stretch of parkland rolling down to the city. By the gate, the blighted tree he had noticed on his first visit had finally died. It lay on its side, the trunk splintered, waiting for the gardener to cut it up for firewood.

"Well, children," he said. "That's it. Time to be going now. It's all over and there's nothing more to worry about." He went to the settee and shook Penny by the arm. "Come on, girl. You've got a car, haven't you? Give your boy friend a lift back to London."

"Yes, I've got a car." She stood up and pulled her coat round her. "Goodbye, General Kirk." She took the hand and then turned to Michael.

"Goodbye, too, Mike. It was good at times, wasn't it, but I'm sorry, no more lifts. My car's quite full up with Glyde family, and we're going alone."

"Penny, listen to me. It's over now. It's all over except for us. That's the only thing that matters now and we've got to go on. Why, I thought—" Michael was on his feet beside her.

"Oh, no, Mike, you didn't think. That's the whole point, you just haven't thought at all. Oh, God, can't you understand. Don't you see what happened? I didn't come here to save you. I just came for him. Right up to the last moment, I came for him. Then I killed him. Mike, I killed my own brother and that woman, and more than that. Much more. Remember what I told you when we first met. Remember I'm the same blood and I may be like him. No, sorry, Mike, but for your sake I can't risk it. This is the end."

"Just shut up and listen to me." Kirk's voice was gruff and angry and came from deep down in his body. "Stop thinking that you're something special and listen. You came here because you were under his spell, just like we were for a moment, but when you saw Michael you woke up. You killed nobody. You acted under my orders, and when you pushed that woman over you were merely revenging your brother. You aren't like him and there's no family. I think he was just something that came into this world by mistake. They occur now and again, people like that, like dwellers of another planet, quite incapable of making an adjustment on this one. Now, stop snivelling and go with Mike.

"And you, Michael. Just take that wounded stag look off your face. You've got nothing to worry about. We may not have come out of this with flying colours, but at least we've beaten it. The three of us have beaten it. And you, you're all right. Whatever she says now, you've got a girl, a damn good girl."

"Yes, sir, as you say, I've got a girl." Michael put his hand on Penny's shoulder and she didn't withdraw from him. Then he led her to the door. "Shall I see you tomorrow, sir?"

"No, not tomorrow. Come in the day after; see you then. Now, get along with you both."

Kirk watched them go out and then picked up the papers on the desk, and slowly went down the steps to the little pink room that lay below.

For quite a long time he sat on the steel chair, turning over the file, then he laid it on the floor and put a match to the corner.

"Well, John," he said, and he wasn't talking to himself. "It's been a long time, hasn't it; but I said I'd get you and here I am." In front of him the paper curled, darkened and glowed to a sudden orange.

"Yes, I've done what I promised, haven't I? But I didn't want it this way. No, I didn't want it like this."

He stood up and very carefully ground the burnt paper to anonymous powder. Then, with a final glance towards the open shutter he went out.

Out of the pink room, with the smell of antiseptic and the mess on the floor waiting for the sweepers. Out through the dark study and the long corridor to his car, with his eyes glassy in the morning light.

Out and back to his stuffy Whitehall office: the fog: the cigar smoke: the telephone beneath his torn hand: the next assignment: a way of life.

THE END